KT-152-206

Heather's Piglets

C016123811

Harry Oulton has worked for Eurodisney in Spain, Coca-Cola in Mexico, made television programmes for both the BBC and ITV, and worked in a factory sticking labels onto boxes. Now he's very happy writing children's books in London, where he lives with his wife and three children. Find out more at www.harryoulton.co.uk or follow him on Twitter @HarryOulton1

The HEATHER series
A Pig Called Heather
The Return of a Pig Called Heather
Heather's Piglets

Heather's Piglets

HARRY OULTON

Piccadilly
PRESS

First published in Great Britain in 2015 by
PICCADILLY PRESS
80-81 Wimpole St, London W1G 9RE
www.piccadillypress.co.uk

Text copyright © Harry Oulton, 2015
Map copyright © Prosper Devas, 2015

All rights reserved.
No part of this publication may be reproduced,
stored or transmitted in any form by any means, electronic,
mechanical, photocopying or otherwise, without the
prior written permission of the publisher.

The right of Harry Oulton to be identified as Author of this
work has been asserted by him in accordance with
the Copyright, Designs and Patents Act, 1988

This is a work of fiction. Names, places, events and
incidents are either the products of the author's imagination or
used fictitiously. Any resemblance to actual persons, living or
dead, or actual events is purely coincidental.

A CIP catalogue record for this book is
available from the British Library.

ISBN: 978–1–848–12479–0
also available as an ebook

1 3 5 7 9 10 8 6 4 2

Typeset in Adobe Caslon Pro 12.5/17pt by
Palimpsest Book Production Limited, Falkirk, Stirlingshire

Printed and bound by Clays Ltd, St Ives Plc

Piccadilly Press is an imprint of Bonnier Publishing Fiction,
a Bonnier Publishing company.
www.bonnierpublishingfiction.co.uk

For Moops and Dot and Fluffy

SCOTLAND

ABERDEEN

THE FORTINGALL YEW

GLASGOW

EDINBURGH

NEWCASTLE

HADRIAN'S WALL

ROUTES TAKEN:
Heather & Aitor
Eder & Tor

SHERWOOD FOREST

ENGLAND

WALES

CARDIFF

BRISTOL

LONDON

N
W   E
S

0   20   40   60   80 100 M
0   40   80   120 160 K

Chapter 1

Morning, Class

The pig called Heather was standing outside the pigsty she called home. It was an ingenious sty/kennel/goatshed combination, especially built for Heather and the other animals by Isla's dad after he moved back to the farm.

Over the last few years, Heather had had several adventures, and along the way had managed to assemble quite a few new friends. So now, in addition to Heather herself, living on the farm were: Rhona the goat; Alastair the sheepdog and his friend Izzy the Jack Russell; Izzy's owner Nikki, who was a human and was more friends with Isla's dad than with the animals; two adolescent piglets, whose names were Tor and Eder and who were Heather's; and eight puppies (Taylor, Chandler, Joey, Ed, Romeo, Rachel, Phoebe and Madonna) belonging to Alastair and Izzy. Add in various chickens and the occasional visits of Katy the Eider duck, and you can see why Mr Wolstenholme had thought they might need a new home.

Heather took a deep breath, and pushed open the door of the sty.

'Morning, love,' she called optimistically as she bustled around straightening straw and pretending to be busy.

There was a groan from the pile of straw in the corner and a bleary, sleepy snout emerged, sniffed the air and went back in again. Heather felt a clutch of pride and love as she always did when she saw her son, Aitor junior. Such a handsome pig, he had her own flaming red colouring, but his father's deep-black, haunted eyes. His father, Aitor senior, had been a Bearded pig crossed with a Basque pig, and in fact Eder, Aitor junior's twin sister, looked far more like her father. She still had the stripes that marked her out as a Bearded piglet, and she was just starting to grow the distinctive beard around her snout.

'T'masleepgoaway,' groaned the pile of straw, and Heather grinned happily as she checked there was water in the trough.

'It's morning, time to get up for school. Rhona was asking after you earlier. She said to me, "Aitor never comes to school these days."'

'Not true,' came an outraged voice from the straw. 'Went yesterday. Anyway, my name's Tor. Can't you just trot off and bother Eder?'

'Eder's been up for ages. Come on. School time.'

Tor groaned and burrowed deeper under the straw.

Heather tutted. 'If your father were here he would tell you how impor—'

'But he's not, is he?' interrupted the piglet, sitting up and looking at his mother. 'He's never been here.

You talk about him, or you used to, but where is he? If he cared about me going to school, he'd be here!'

Heather looked down sadly at Aitor junior. Her brown eyes were suddenly a bit watery, and Tor knew he'd gone too far.

He stood up and gave her a nudge. 'Okay, okay, I'll go to school.'

Heather left him to it. But her mood was spoiled and she wanted to be somewhere else. Somewhere she wouldn't be reminded of things she wanted to forget. She strode purposefully away from the sty in no particular direction. It wasn't Tor's fault, but talking about Aitor senior had made her all thinky. Her son was right. Where was his father? Why wasn't he here?

'Heather!' called a voice.

Heather sighed. It was Rhona the goat.

'What are you doing here?' asked Rhona.

Heather looked around. Her walking had brought her to the ruined castle by Isla's vegetable patch. There was the medlar tree that provided the fruit for Isla's dad's jelly-making business, and the little stream, where she and Isla had used to skim stones, long ago.

'Please go away. I'm trying not to think.'

'So I see,' answered the goat. 'About anything in particular?'

Realising she wasn't going to be able to avoid talking to her oldest friend, Heather sighed. 'Yes. I'm trying not to think about something and it's really hard, so instead of trying not to think about that one thing, I'm trying my best to think about lots of other things. And those other things are Isla.'

'Isla?'

'Yes, my friend Isla. I was going through all the birthday parties she's had. I've got to the one where Farmer Wolstenholme used the tractor to build her a fort out of hay bales.'

'That was her sixth, wasn't it?'

'Yes. She and that nice girl Millie were allowed to stay up really late in the hay-bale fort. I did too. We had a midnight feast. They had chocolate biscuits and I had four apples.' *Gavins, a nice mixture of sweet and sharp. An under-rated apple.*

Isla was at big school now, so she didn't see Heather as much as she used to when they were best friends.

'Why are you thinking about Isla?' asked Rhona. 'Are you missing her?'

Heather looked sad. 'I always miss her, but actually that wasn't why I was thinking about her. I told you, there's a thought I don't want to think, so to avoid thinking it I'm thinking about things which it isn't.'

Rhona raised an eyebrow. 'Okay, if you say so. I've got a favour to ask. Izzy's having her new litter a bit early and needs some help, so there's nobody to teach at school this afternoon. Could you do it?'

Heather looked at her friend in panic. Her? Teach a class? At school! She couldn't be a proper teacher! 'I can't!' she blurted. 'I'm really busy!'

Her goat friend raised the other eyebrow.

Heather looked desperate. 'I am! I've got to . . .' She racked her brains and when she saw a tractor inspiration struck. 'I said I'd help Isla with her homework. She's doing a thing on things that move around farms with motors and wheels . . .' Heather petered out. Given that Isla was thirteen, at big school, a human and not actually there, this was a rubbish excuse even by Heather's standards. Rhona didn't even acknowledge it.

'They're waiting by the barn.'

'What about Alastair?' asked Heather in desperation.

'He did PE with them this morning, and anyway I think he wants to be with Izzy when she has her puppies. I would do it, but I did Roman history with them yesterday and I've got to prepare for tomorrow, so it's down to you. Go on, it'll be fun. See you later.'

The goat trotted off and Heather groaned and buried her head between her trotters. It wasn't that she minded helping Rhona out – after all, the clever goat was teaching her piglets, and so really it was the least Heather could do. It was more *who* she was going to be teaching that was the problem.

It was Tor.

And then it happened. The thought that Heather had been trying to avoid came barging into her head, pushed all the other thoughts out of the way and plonked itself down right behind Heather's deep-brown eyes.

Aitor. Big Aitor. The blind father of Eder and Tor, the only pig Heather had ever really loved. Where was he now? Was he even alive? It was a huge, difficult, painful thought and she didn't want to think it.

Heather shook her snout from side to side in a vain attempt to empty her head, but it was no good. She gave in, closed her eyes and started to really remember him, to wallow in the memories of his stories, his wisdom, his terrible jokes. How she longed to see him again, to be laughed at, teased and nudged. How she longed to be called 'Eder' again, the Basque word for 'pretty', and his special name for her, so personal that she couldn't bear to lose it, so she'd given it to their daughter. Why wasn't he here, sharing the everyday joys and frustrations of being a parent to two adolescent piglets?

The piglets! Rhona! School! She'd forgotten all about them! Heather lurched to her feet and set off at a fast(ish) trot for the barn.

The class was getting restless. Joey the puppy and Tor the piglet were pretending to be war pigs, and Tor's sister Eder was chatting to Taylor, Joey's big sister. A young chick, who had only started school a few weeks earlier, came over, her head bobbing nervously.

'Where's the teacher? Is she nae coming?' she clucked.

Eder looked at her. 'Rhona? Don't worry, she'll be here soon.'

'But she's late,' said the chick. 'She's never late. We'll not have time to do everything.'

'Enjoy it,' replied Taylor, discreetly tapping the side of her head with one paw to show Eder she thought the chick was a bit off her feed.

'Look! Someone's coming, but it isnae Rhona,' said the relieved chick, happily looking down the path.

Everyone turned to see Heather trotting towards them and Tor groaned.

'Oh no, it's Mother. What does she want?'

'Mebbe she's a supply teacher?' suggested the chick.

'Hello, everyone,' said Heather nervously as she arrived.

'Hi, Mum,' answered Eder happily. 'Are you our teacher?'

'Just for today,' answered Heather. 'Izzy's having

her puppies.' She sat down in front of them, unsure exactly what to do next. 'Um . . .'

'Normally Rhona takes the register?' whispered Eder.

'Of course! The register. Right. That is . . . ?'

'When you check who's here?'

Heather looked puzzled. 'But I can see who's here.'

'It's just what you do, Mum, to make sure nobody's bunking off. Call out our names and we answer.'

'Okay.' Heather tried to look important. 'Eder Ezkurra-Duroc!'

'Here, Mum. But you're probably okay just with the first name.'

Heather looked worried. 'What if there's two Eders?'

'Then you use the first letter of the surname. So I'd be Eder E.'

Heather looked relieved. 'I see. Right, let's carry on. Taylor D?'

'Present,' answered the little puppy. 'But there's only one Taylor so you don't need to use my surname.'

Heather leant forward to the young chicken. 'I'm sorry, I don't know your name.'

'I'm Kirstie Macgillivray,' answered the chick eagerly. 'Will you be teaching us more numeracy?'

Heather looked a bit alarmed. 'Let's just finish the register first, shall we?' She looked around. 'Joey?'

The puppy loudly barked his presence.

Heather took a deep breath. 'Aitor?'

No answer.

'Aitor?'

Still no answer. Heather stared straight at the arrogant piglet who was grinning back at her.

'Aitor. Could you say your name for the register please?'

'Of course, Mother. But you haven't asked me yet.'

Heather sighed. '*Tor* Ezkurra-Duroc?'

The piglet bowed low. 'Present, Mother dearest.'

Everyone giggled and even Heather had to smile as her son tried his best to look serious.

'Right, let's get started.'

Kirstie's wing shot up in the air, frantically quivering, with the other one placed over her beak to stop herself speaking.

'Yes, Kirstie?'

'You didn't call me out in the register. Only Rhona said we'd get a gold star if we had perfect attendance and I don't want to miss out.'

Heather looked at her fondly. What a nice chick, and so hard-working. She shuddered as she remembered the chicks she'd freed from Mr Busby's factory, back when the farm had been a chicken farm.

'Kirstie M?'

'Present!' clucked the chick happily.

'So, why don't you tell me what you were all doing last lesson?' asked Heather. 'Kirstie?'

The chick stood up. 'Well, first Miss Rhona told us all about how the Roman Empire was huge, and how they used to use animals to fight, like tortoises.'

'Tortoises? Really?' Heather was intrigued. Fortunately Eder's hand went up. 'Yes, Eder?' said Heather.

'She means the Roman soldiers formed a shell with shields over their heads and by the sides of their bodies so the enemy's arrows couldn't get through. It was called a tortoise.'

'Oh, I see,' replied Heather, relieved. She glanced around at all the little faces looking at her expectantly, so eager to learn. All except one . . .

'Tor? Anything else?'

'Fractions,' answered the young pig, staring at her. 'Actually, I wanted to ask a question, please? If you have one apple and you bite it in half, does it then become two apples, or is it one apple but split into two halves?'

Heather looked at him. 'That would depend,' she answered crossly. Why was he testing her?

'On what?' grinned Tor.

'On whether you'd eaten one of the halves when you bit the apple in two. If you had it wouldn't be a half any more because there would only be one of it. You cannot have only one half of something.'

She paused for a second, as something else had occurred to her. She looked at Tor.

'Also, which bit of you ate the half-apple? Was it the half of you that comes from me? The Duroc pig half? Or the half of you which is half Bearded pig and half Basque pig? Because if it was your Basque half you wouldn't have eaten it because you'd have wanted an acorn instead, but if it was your Duroc half you would probably have eaten all the apple and that would be the end of that.'

Nice answer, said a deep voice in the back of Heather's head. Around her everyone was laughing and chatting away about Tor being so many different types of pig. But Heather wasn't listening. She hadn't heard that voice for a long time. She held up her trotter for silence.

'Okay, that's class over for today. Go and play.'

Everyone whooped and jumped up, except for Kirstie who looked like she was about to burst into tears. 'But we've nae learnt anything! Och, I feel as stupid and ignorant as I did when I came here this morning. Can you nae teach us something else?'

Heather looked at her. 'Your homework is to work out three ways to tell which direction is north.' Heather set off purposefully towards the farm.

'Where are you going?' asked Kirstie in despair.

'To see a dog about a man.'

Chapter 2

Take Me to the River . . .

Heather knew where she'd find Izzy. Whenever any of the animals were having babies they always went under the barn. There was a sort of nest of hay where Rhona kept old books she hadn't yet had a chance to devour, and it was always comfortable, safe and warm.

Sure enough, when Heather crawled under the barn there was the little celebrity-obsessed Jack Russell who either talked and talked and talked or just said 'yup'. She was lying down on a rug, her tummy looking very full of puppies. Alastair, her sheepdog partner, was driving her nuts, so she was actually quite pleased to see Heather.

'Hi, Heather, thanks for doing the lesson. How was it, what did you do?'

'We did this thing called the register and then fractions. You know, bits of what and who. Looks like your puppies are coming.'

'Yup.'

Heather paused. She wasn't quite sure how to say what she wanted to say. But Izzy was a mum, so perhaps she'd understand.

'Have you noticed anything about Tor? I mean, anything unusual?'

'You mean, why he's so rude to you? Why you keep fighting? He always seems to not want to see you? But then sometimes is really loving? That sort of thing?'

Heather nodded. 'Is it that obvious?'

'Yup.'

Heather sighed. 'This morning when I woke him

up he told me to trot off, cheeky boy. But then last week he couldn't have been sweeter. He brought me ten different types of apple and bet me I couldn't taste them all and say what they were without looking. Honestly, I don't know which way's up.'

'You must have won that bet easily,' scoffed Izzy. 'What was the prize?'

'An apple,' said Heather happily. Then she looked sad. 'He was the loveliest little piglet. Really affectionate and funny. And now . . .' She petered out.

Izzy looked thoughtful as her tummy churned, the puppies inside getting ready to come out. 'He's growing up. Finding his own identity. You know? His thing, his own space. He's the same Tor, but he's changing from piglet to pig. You must have had piglets before?'

Heather shook her head. 'When I was a working pig all my litters were taken away and sold when they were small. I've never really had a piglet who was older than six months. Are they often like this?'

'Yup.'

Heather waited for Izzy to go on, but she didn't.

So Heather did. 'But Eder isn't like that. She isn't rude. Or naughty. Nor are your puppies. Taylor's a gem.'

Izzy rolled onto her back and tried to get comfy. Alastair was fussing around and she looked exasperatedly at him. She turned her head back to Heather.

'Different personalities do it in different ways. Some rebel, some lie, some get grumpy. Also, I'm not famous. Tor's the son of a celebrity, so that means he has to struggle even harder to be himself.'

'Celebrity? You mean me?' asked a bemused Heather.

'Yup.'

'But I'm not famous any more – these days I'm just a Duroc again.'

'But you were a super-celebrity.' Izzy turned to Alastair, who was sitting really close to her and looking more and more worried. 'Alastair, love, could you get me some water?' Thankful for something to do, Alastair tore off out of the nest and Izzy turned back to Heather. 'You travelled all over Britain and you saved the farm. You were on posters all over the place, and you were almost on TV. How is a young piglet going to make his way in the world if he always sees himself as Heather's piglet, rather than an animal in his own right?'

Alastair arrived back in the barn, his tongue hanging out as he panted, 'Forgot the bowl.' He picked it up and raced off again.

Heather rested her snout on her trotters. 'And you really think that's the problem?'

'Yup.'

'What do I do? I can't make myself un-famous in the past.'

'Pass me that blanket.'

Heather was relieved. That was easy. 'This one?'

'Yup.'

Heather grabbed the blanket in her mouth and dragged it over to Izzy. 'There. So will that make little Tor into a nice piglet?'

Izzy shook her head. 'No. But I don't want my puppies to get chilly.' She stretched out on the blanket.

Alastair reappeared, pushing the water bowl and carrying a big bone in his mouth, and for the next couple of hours Heather watched in happy awe as he helped Izzy give birth to four tiny boy puppies who she called John, Paul, George and Ringo. As Alastair licked them clean and then positioned them so their mum could feed them, all the while fussing around Izzy and making sure she was comfortable and happy, the thought that had been nagging away at Heather came back, complete with its new bit, and demanded to be thought.

'Izzy?'

Izzy was gnawing at the bone Alastair had brought so her mouth was a bit full. 'Ymmmmp.'

'A very weird thing just happened to me. I heard a voice in my head that I haven't heard for a long time. And it reminded me of something that I've been meaning to ask you.'

The dog looked intrigued.

Heather took a deep breath. 'Do you remember that man who Nikki – your Nikki, who used to look after me when they were trying to get me to be an advertisement and who is now sort of friends with Isla's dad – used to work with?'

The little dog chewed while she translated what Heather had just said. Then she nodded and swallowed.

'Mr Hornbuckle. Funny man. Nikki always said his heart was in the right place. He's a chicken control supervisor now. What about him?'

Heather took a deep breath. She had never thought this far before and she was a bit nervous that once she actually said what she was thinking, she wouldn't be able to un-say it. Once it was voiced, it wasn't just a thought any more, it was a solid thing, and there was no turning back. Like a song that doesn't really exist until you sing it. She closed her eyes tightly and spoke all in a rush.

'Did he ever tell you whether he found Aitor? I mean, did he catch him and return him to the zoo or did he never find him? Because he ended up coming to the farm so he must have realised that I wasn't with Aitor any more and he would only have known that if he found him, but if he did find him then what did he do with him and if he didn't find him why did he come to the farm unless he couldn't find him but he thought this was where I'd come because he didn't really want Aitor at all it was me he was after and anyway there's no way he would have known that we'd separated and also he was right about me coming back here because I did and so did he and I suppose what I really want to know is did he ever say anything to Nikki about Aitor being dead?'

'Yup.'

That was that. Heather was devastated. Her ears flopped over her eyes and her heart turned over with a horrible lurch. Suddenly everything was pressing down on her and she felt worse than she'd ever felt. This was why she hated thinking! Why had she asked the question? If that thought hadn't been such a bully and forced its way to the front of her head she would never have had to find out.

'Actually, it's yes, but also no,' said Izzy thoughtfully. 'I mean, yes, Mr Hornbuckle did talk to Nikki about Aitor, but no, he didn't say if he'd caught him or not. He assumed he was dead, but he didn't actually know for definite. I think he was a bit embarrassed that he'd chased a pig underground for so long and had nothing to show for it. In fact, thinking about it I'm sure he would have told us if he had. Or maybe not? He was quite a secretive man. Private and a bit strange. So maybe the answer should have been "no". Why d'you ask?'

Heather's heart was beating again. Actually beating faster than ever before. Suddenly thoughts and plans were flooding into her head in an excited rush. Her head was getting very full so she opened her mouth to let some of the thoughts out.

'Everyone Aitor I find am to tell going you will?' And she galloped out of the barn.

Izzy nodded. 'Yup.'

At that point Alastair came back in pushing an old apple crate full of straw.

'What's up with Heather? It's been a while since I've seen her move that fast.' He started to pick up the snoozing puppies and put them into the crate.

'She's going to look for Aitor.'

Heather gathered up as many apples as she could find for the journey and put them in a pile. They were a mixture of *Feltham Beauty, an early-season apple with*

a melting, sweet flesh, and *Malling, greenish-yellow with a crisp white aromatic flesh*. It was a good selection and her mouth watered as she looked at them. Lunch seemed a long time ago. In fact, had she actually had lunch at all? Still, she had more important things to do now. She separated the apples out into two piles. She had ten *Feltham Beauties* and nine *Mallings*. That was no good. She could either go and find another *Malling* or eat one of the *Feltham Beauties*. She didn't have time to go hunting so she quickly ate one up. Weirdly, that made her hungrier, so to balance things out she ate a *Malling*. Only that didn't balance things out. Now they were different again. Bother! Why was it always so complicated?

What was it Tor had said about fractions. A bitten apple was two halves of one apple? That might work. She took a bite out of one of the *Feltham Beauties* and then counted them up again. Still the same. Nine *Feltham Beauties* (one with a bite taken out) and eight *Mallings*. Why hadn't it worked? Hopefully, she took a bite out of each of the remaining apples but that didn't work either.

These apples were supposed to be for her journey, and now they all had bits missing. They'd go brown. Heather didn't mind brown apples generally, but they weren't as nice as crisp ones with unbroken skins. There was only one thing to do. So she did it, and was lying down feeling rather full when Rhona appeared.

'Izzy says you're going to look for Aitor?'

Heather looked sad. 'I was going to, but I've made a mess of things.'

'What have you done?'

'I've eaten all the apples I'd found for the journey and I haven't even left yet. How am I going to find him if I can't even manage that?'

'Why have you suddenly decided to look for him?'

Heather paused. It was really hard to explain. She wasn't even sure she knew precisely, but it was just a thing – a nagging thought that he was out there, and she was here, and that wasn't right.

'Is it Tor? Are you worried about him?' asked the goat.

Heather thought about that as well. In part it was Tor, but it wasn't worry that was nagging at her.

'Yes, but it's Eder too. It's not that I'm worried – it's more that I'm proud. And I know he would be too. He's missing out because he's not here, and if he's not here it's because he can't be, so I need to find him and help him and bring him back here. I think.'

Rhona nodded. 'That makes sense. But I have to ask you this. What if he's not . . . alive?'

Heather shrugged. 'Then I've lost nothing by looking.' She paused for a second. 'He used to say something to me, when we were travelling.

If you see an apple on a chair,

It's likely someone put it there.

Apparently it's an old Basque proverb.'

Rhona looked intrigued. 'And do you understand it? Is that what's made up your mind?'

'Absolutely not,' said Heather, shaking her head emphatically. 'No idea what it means at all. But it would be nice to know. So when I find him, I shall ask him.'

Heather paused for a minute, gathering her thoughts, and then looked straight at Rhona. 'He said to me a long time ago that he wanted to see the Northern Lights before he died. I told him that might be tricky, what with him being blind and all, but he just laughed, and said he'd be sure to have me with him so I could describe them. I'm feeling it's nearly time to take that trip.'

At that point Eder raced round the corner, her eyes wide open in fear and her ears flat against her head.

'Mum! Mum! Come quick! It's Joey! He's in the pool!'

'What do you mean?'

'We were all playing by the pool, and Tor was daring him to walk along a branch, and Joey slipped and now he's in the pool and he can't swim and we can't get to him and he's – he's – he's—'

Heather jumped to her feet. Apples and Aitor were forgotten as she interrupted her daughter and shouted instructions.

'Go and find Alastair. Now! He's with Izzy in the barn.' She turned to Rhona. 'Go and fetch Isla, and get her to come to the quarry. I'll go and see what's happening.'

As Rhona galloped off towards the farmhouse, Heather raced to the pool as fast as she could. The pool was at the bottom of a small disused quarry, which had been abandoned years before and had slowly filled up with water, so now it was an excellent swimming hole. The whole thing was about twenty metres wide, and it was quite deep so it was a great place to bathe in the summer. But if you weren't a confident swimmer it could be very dangerous – there was almost nowhere to put your feet down, and the puppies and the piglets knew they were never allowed to go there without a grownup.

When Heather arrived she was panting and gasping for breath. Kirstie the chicken, Taylor, and two other puppies were all jumping up and down on the bank, trying to peer in and see what was happening. Tor was in the water, swimming around frantically.

'He's in here!' shouted Tor, pointing to the middle of the pool with his trotter. 'He fell in and he went underwater! I can't see him!'

Heather didn't hesitate. She took a huge breath and leapt into the middle of the pool. The initial jump took her underwater and she opened her eyes and peered into the depths of the pool, trying to see the puppy. But the water was murky and she couldn't see anything. She put her head above water. 'Where did he go in?' she asked.

'Here! Here!' shouted Tor. On the side nearest the farm was a tree with a branch that stretched out across the pool. Tor pointed to it. 'He was trying to balance on the branch and he fell into the pool.'

Heather took another deep breath and dived down under the water. She tried to swim down but it was impossible to see anything. She kicked out with all four legs and drove herself down towards the bottom. There! She saw Joey. The puppy was trapped in some weeds at the very bottom of the pool. As she looked she thought she could see him wriggling, but he looked like he was losing strength and it was too far for her to swim down.

She swam back up and gasped in more air. She crawled out onto the bank.

'I can see him,' she panted, 'but he's trapped at the bottom. Have to get deeper.' She galloped to the bank and ran up to the top of the quarry. In the distance Heather could see Alastair tearing over the field followed by Eder, but he was too far away. She couldn't wait. She took two steps back, took a huge breath, galloped to the edge of the quarry and plummeted down into the pool.

She almost had no time to feel scared as she dropped like a stone, the air being forced out of her lungs as she went down, down, into the depths of the pool, deeper and deeper, turning from side to side as she tried to catch sight of the little puppy. There! He was about a metre away, completely tangled in the weeds and unable to escape. His eyes were closed and he hung, still and lifeless.

Heather kicked out with all four trotters and swam towards him. The water was churning all around her, pulling her back as she struggled to reach him. Her lungs were burning but she drove on and finally got to him. She tried to loosen the weeds but they were bound tight. She shook him and his eyes opened. He looked terrified and she clutched at him, frantically trying to free him from the weeds. Her lungs were on fire as she was desperate for air, but the little puppy was totally trapped. She had to get him out!

She redoubled her efforts as her head started to pound, the blood roaring in her brain and her eyes starting to cloud over as the puppy drifted in and out of focus. She had untangled most of the weeds now but the effort was using up more and more air and her lungs were burning. One last tough length of weed held him down, and wouldn't be untangled. She'd have to bite it, but that meant opening her mouth. Underwater!

She had no choice. She opened her mouth and chewed at the stubborn weed. Water was pouring down her throat and into her tummy as she finally cut through the weed. Far above her the water exploded as Alastair arrived and dived into the pool. With the last of her strength Heather pushed the little puppy up towards his father, and then she closed her eyes and gave up. The last thought she had before she lost consciousness was that the weeds tasted a bit like cabbage.

Chapter 3

The Sty's the Limit . . .

Isla was listening to her iPod when Rhona arrived breathless at the farmhouse. She was texting someone on her phone and also doing her homework, which meant she was Skyping Millie on her computer to get help with a maths problem. Given all that, it was hardly surprising she didn't hear the bleating goat, or see her jumping up and down outside her bedroom window.

'So a power set is a subset of all the other sets?' asked Isla.

'No, a power set is a set of all the subsets of one set. Isn't that Rhona behind you?' answered Millie.

Isla looked round at the precise moment Rhona dropped below the level of the window, so she didn't see anything.

'The goat? Don't think so. A set of all the subsets of the set? Cool.'

Behind her Rhona jumped up again bleating and Millie burst out laughing.

'It is her! Go to the window.'

Isla put down the phone, turned round and walked over to the window. Right as she got there the goat bounced up and bleated frantically. Isla jumped in shock.

'What's up? Wait there. I'll come outside.'

Ever since Rhona had written in the dirt the day she and her dad got the farm back, Isla had always had suspicions that there was a lot more to Rhona than your average goat, so she looked at her seriously when she came out of the house.

'Are you okay?'

Rhona bit Isla's jersey and pulled.

'Will I come with you?'

Rhona galloped off, and Isla bent down, tied the laces on her shiny red DMs, and then ran after the speeding goat.

By the pool it was mayhem. Alastair was frantically licking Joey and blowing into his mouth. The others were peering into the water looking for Heather, who hadn't emerged.

Rhona and Isla arrived and seeing the puppy and Tor frantic in the water the girl quickly worked out someone was in the pool. Within seconds she had dived in and hauled and pushed Heather onto the bank. She'd called her dad who'd come quickly round with the quad bike and together they heaved Heather on board and took her back to the farmhouse.

By the time the others got back, Heather was lying unconscious, but breathing, in Isla's bedroom in the farmhouse with Isla, her dad and the vet all gathered around her. Rhona sidled over to the window to listen to what was being said, and about half an hour later she came back to where all the others were gathered. She looked grim.

'It's not disastrous, but it's not that good either. There was loads of muddy water in her lungs and they think she may have got a chest infection.'

'What does that mean?' asked Izzy.

'We won't know until she's come round properly, but it's not good. The vet was very gloomy, but Isla was so brave and wouldn't allow him to say anything negative. How's Joey – is he okay?'

'Yup.' Izzy pointed to the corner where Joey was curled up, fast asleep.

Rhona was still looking worried. 'Eder is by the farmhouse in case Heather wakes up, but where's Tor? Has anyone seen him?'

Izzy shook her head. 'Probably staying out of Alastair's way.'

'Why? Was he . . . involved?" asked Rhona tentatively.

'Yup.' The little dog shifted so her new puppies could latch on and start suckling. She looked cross. 'I know Joey can be stupid. I mean, he didn't *have* to walk on that branch. But apparently Tor dared him? You know how Joey worships him. He'd jump off a cliff if Tor told him to.'

Rhona nodded. 'But he'd never mean him any harm; he loves Joey so much.'

Izzy sighed. 'Sometimes love isn't enough.' Then she shuddered and re-arranged herself. 'I just can't help thinking . . . if Heather hadn't jumped in and got him . . . ?'

'But she did. And he's safe now. I'm sure Alastair won't take his eyes off him for a minute.'

Izzy nodded. 'He wants to teach them all how to swim. Says it's time they learnt. One thing. I know Tor will be feeling guilty, but don't forget Eder. She'll be worried sick about her mum.'

Rhona walked all over the farm looking for the missing boy piglet but couldn't find any sign of him anywhere. Eventually she gave up and went and found Eder, who was sitting outside the farmhouse under Isla's window. In front of her were two pears.

'What's up?' asked Rhona.

Eder was staring at the fruit. 'Mum had started

cataloguing pears as well as apples, so I thought I'd carry on so that when she got better she didn't have as much to do.'

'That's helpful of you.'

The little piglet was close to tears. 'But I can't do it! One of these is a *Conference* and the other's a *Concorde* and I don't know which is which! There are so many types and how am I going to catalogue all the rest of them when I can't even tell a *Conference* from a *Concorde!*'

Eder's piglet stripes had all but disappeared, and the first little tufts of beard were growing around her snout, but she still seemed very young, especially when she was worried.

Rhona sat down next to her. 'The *Concorde* is more widely grown, but the *Conference* apparently has an infinitely better flavour. I say *apparently* because I have to confess that to me they taste pretty similar. I know the *Conference* was introduced into Britain in 1885 by a man called Thomas Rivers. But I only know that because I've read it. So, do they taste different?'

The piglet snuffled. 'Of course. That one's far crisper. It's sweeter. More pineapple in it. In fact, it's almost tropical. Plus it has a darker skin tone. But that's the point! I can't remember which it is. How does Mum do it?'

'You will. In time,' smiled the goat. 'Your mother has an extraordinary ability to differentiate between apples, but she's built it up over years. How many apples do you think she's eaten in her life?'

'Like a million?' answered Eder, the first signs of a grin appearing on her face.

'Two million, I'd have thought,' laughed Rhona. 'Stop worrying, Eder. Hopefully your mother will be back enjoying apples and pears before you can say *Golden Delicious*. By the way, any idea where your brother might be?'

'Sorry, 'fraid not,' lied Eder.

'I hope he's okay, and not too scared of Alastair. I imagine he's as upset about his mum as you are, but he probably shows it in a different way.'

'Like by being horrible to her?'

'Do you know what a cliché is?' asked Rhona.

'Is it something that has been said like a zillion times?'

'Exactly. Usually because it's true. Like "the early bird gets the worm". Anyway, there is another one: "You always hurt the one you love".'

Eder nodded. 'That'd be Tor.'

Rhona looked sideways at the piglet. 'You know she was going to look for your dad?'

'Dad? Mum? I thought he was dead.'

'She seems to think not. When you came and found her she was getting ready to set off. Gathering apples, so she'd have something to eat on the journey.'

Eder looked confused. 'But . . . what about us? I mean, me and Tor?'

'Maybe she didn't think you needed looking after any more? Maybe she thinks you're both old enough to be responsible?'

Eder snorted. 'She got that wrong then, didn't she?'

'Did she?' replied Rhona thoughtfully. 'I think she knows you better than you think.' She paused for a second, 'Anyway, doesn't matter any more, does it?'

'What do you mean?'

'Well, she won't be going anywhere for a while, so it's irrelevant. Shame, I think she was really looking forward to seeing your dad again.' The goat looked at the little pig; she could almost hear Eder's brain racing.

Rhona smiled to herself as she headed off. She looked back as she went. 'Oh, and Eder, if someone was going to go off and maybe look for another someone . . . ?' Eder nodded and Rhona carried on, 'they might want to get a move on. Understand?'

'No. What do you mean?'

'I mean . . . well, your mum may not have all the time in the world.'

Rhona watched as Eder worked out that she was talking about Heather being very ill.

'But you said she was going to be . . . ? Oh, I see,' said Eder bravely, 'you were being nice to me.' She stood up and bravely squared her shoulders. 'Right. How long have we got?'

Rhona shrugged. 'Just find him.'

Eder waited until she was sure she was alone before she went to find Tor. She suspected he'd be in the small quarry, so that's where she started looking. The small quarry must have once been part of the big one, but now they were both underwater you had to swim to get to the smaller one. Tor had found the entrance when he'd been exploring one day, and apart from his sister he'd told no one about it. It was his own secret place and Eder was fairly sure that's where she'd find him.

She swam confidently through the large quarry, dived under the water and emerged into the small one. Sure enough, she could make out a figure sitting right by the far edge where the old quarry workings had been. It was Tor, and he looked miserable. She gave the hoot of an owl which was their signal to each other, but the figure didn't react or even acknowledge her.

Up to the right there was a sort of bit of rock that jutted out, and if you balanced on it you could speak and the sound echoed around the quarry like a weird microphone. Eder didn't like it because the ledge was so small and it felt really dangerous, but she plucked up her courage and clambered up.

She tried to stick as close to the wall as she could

and then cleared her throat before speaking. Her voice echoed around the chamber. 'There's a man in a cinema and he notices a pig sitting further down the aisle watching the film. So he shuffles along and says, "Excuse me, aren't you a pig?" "Yes," replies the pig, not taking his eyes off the screen. "So what are you doing at the cinema?" asked the man.'

Eder paused and waited for Tor to guess the punchline of the joke, but he was silent, so she scrambled down to the floor and then trotted over towards him.

'Thought I'd find you here.'

'That's the trouble with having a sister. Suppose you told everyone where I was.'

'Course not!' said Eder indignantly. 'Figured you wanted to be alone for a bit or you wouldn't have disappeared.'

'How's Mum?' asked Tor. He sounded casual but Eder knew better.

'Alive. Just. She's sleeping in Isla's bed. They're waiting for her to wake up.'

'She'll be fine.'

'No thanks to you.'

'I didn't ask her to dive in.'

'Someone had to save Joey.'

Tor was silent.

Eder looked at him crossly. 'You're an idiot. You know Joey does everything you tell him to. What were you thinking?'

'Well, it wasn't just me – we were *all* there! Why didn't you stop him?' snapped Tor.

'I shouldn't have to!' Eder shook her head. Sometimes, her brother was impossible. She turned and headed back off across the little quarry. She called back as she went, 'Alastair's really cross with you. I think you should avoid him for a bit.'

'How do you suggest I do that? This farm's so small. I can't stand it!'

'I don't really care. Go away somewhere. Go and look for Dad.'

'Look for Dad? Are you out of your sty?' Tor was incredulous.

Eder stopped at the foot of the rocks you had to swim under to get back to the large quarry. 'Yeah. Aitor. Your father. Our dad.'

'But he's dead.'

'Mum thinks not. She was going to look for him.'

'Rubbish.'

'Okay.' Eder started walking into the water.

Tor got up and trotted towards her. 'Wait. What could possibly make you think I would want anything to do with someone I don't know and who has never shown any interest in me my whole life?'

'Hmm, let's see. Maybe, just for once, I thought you might be able to consider doing something that wasn't just for you. Clearly I was wrong.' Eder shook her snout crossly, and carried on getting deeper.

'Stop!' The word echoed off the walls as her brother called after her.

Eder ignored him and took a deep breath, ready to dive under.

'Eder! Wait up . . . please?'

It was the 'please' that made her stop. She looked back and saw Tor standing at the edge of the pool, his trotters in the water, looking at her.

'At least tell me what happened to the pig?'

'Eh?'

'In the joke. The man asks, "What are you doing at the cinema?"'

Eder smiled as she swam back. 'The pig says, "I really liked the book."'

Tor grinned back at her. 'Nice one. By the way, what do you mean, do something not for me?'

'Mum was going to find Dad before she— Anyway, now she can't. And it's kind of your fault. So, I thought maybe you could go instead?'

Tor looked at his sister. How could he explain to her that it was different for him? How could he make her see that while she could be like their mother, he didn't have a dad to model himself on. He was on his own. He wanted a dad more than anything, but he wanted a dad who wanted him. A dad who wanted to be there. How do you even begin to say that?

He shook his head. 'I can't.'

'Why not?'

'You wouldn't understand.'

'Try me.'

He thought about it a bit more. Actually, why couldn't he go? What did he have to lose? He grinned at his sister. 'If I go, you'll have to come too. Chum me?'

Eder looked at her brother. How could she explain to him that she was absolutely terrified of finding her father? Of being a disappointment to him? Of not being . . . her mother? How could she make him see that for her, meeting her dad might just be the hardest thing in the world?

'I can't.'

'Why not? Mum's got Isla, I'm sure Taylor can talk to someone else about girl stuff, so you're free to come with me.'

'It's hard to explain.'

'Come on, Little Miss Words. You're always top in class. Tell me.'

She thought about it. Actually, what was she so scared of? Fear only had power if you let it. She took a deep breath and grinned back at him. 'Sure you want me?'

'Are you going to be bossy?'

'I *am* your big sister.'

'By like a minute.'

'Fact remains I was born first, which makes me older, which gives me certain responsibilities. Technically it puts me in charge.'

'So that's a yes to the bossiness then.'

'I think it makes sense for one of us to take charge of leadership, yes.'

'Fair. So where is he?'

'Who?'

'Our father. Where is he? Where are we going?'

'He's . . . in England.'

'Yeah. Where exactly?'

'How should I know?'

'Because you're in charge.'

'Only in charge of leading. And planning.'

'So not of knowing everything.'

'Course not.'

'Because I know where he is.'

'Do not!'

'Do so.'

'Do not!' shouted Eder indignantly.

'No. You're right. I don't. But nor do you. So who died and made you queen-pig?'

'Fine! We'll be a democracy.'

'A what?'

'A democracy. A state of political or social equality. Means actually nobody's in charge. We vote on stuff or just agree.'

Tor looked sceptical. 'But there's only two of us. We'd just vote against each other. Sounds like a disaster. What's the thing where the most athletic, sporty one is in charge? The law of something?'

'The law of the jungle. Rule of the fittest. Otherwise known as tyranny.'

'*Tor*-anny. I like that. Much easier. We can just do what I say.'

Eder shook her head. 'But I'm so much cleverer than you.'

'But I'm more handsome and charming. You've got a ridiculous tufty beard.'

'It's not ridiculous!' squeaked Eder crossly. 'You're just jealous, and jealousy is not attractive.'

'Nor is a beard on a pig. Specially not a tufty one.'

The two piglets were grinning at each other.

'You scared?' asked Aitor.

'Terrified,' replied Eder. 'You?'

'Actually, I'm more scared of Alastair catching up with me. Why do you think I agreed to go?'

'So we are going then?' asked Eder.

Tor looked determined. 'First democratic decision.' He raised a trotter. 'I propose, whatever else we do, we do not tell Joey.'

Eder raised a trotter with him. 'Agreed. Definitely not, motion carried.'

Chapter 4

War Pigs . . .

By midnight the three of them were on the road heading south towards England.

Unsurprisingly, the departure hadn't been quite as smooth as Tor and Eder had planned. They'd stayed in the quarry until sunset, by which time they reckoned everyone would be asleep, and then the two of them had walked up out of the quarry and headed back towards the farm. Eder had gone about ten metres before she realised her brother wasn't with her. She went back and found him sitting on his haunches.

'What's up?' asked Eder.

Her brother was staring at the familiar shape of Bennachie, a mountain which soared proudly up from the fields, about a mile north of the farm. Eder sat next to him and looked at the familiar sight of the mountain. The peak was sloped on one side and then sheer on the other, almost as if a giant were lying down for a snooze, his nose sticking up in the air.

'Just weird to think about leaving,' answered Tor. 'I always thought that every day I'd wake up and pretty much the first thing I'd see would be *Mons Graupius*.'

'Eh?' said Eder.

'*Mons Graupius* is what the Romans used to call Bennachie. Rhona was telling us the other day – but I think you missed the lesson. You know this is the farthest north the Romans ever came. There was a massive battle right here, between them and the Scots.'

Eder looked interested. 'Romans? Really? But that must have been like years ago.'

'Rhona said it was nearly two thousand years ago. The Caledonii were the last unconquered British tribe. They knew they'd lose in a full battle against the Romans so they always avoided it.'

'What happened?'

Tor looked sad. 'The Romans waited until they'd got the harvest into the grain stores and then they attacked the stores. They started destroying them and that forced us to actually meet them in battle.'

'Sneaky. Did we win?'

'No. We were thrashed. The Romans had armour and they were better organised than we were. They reckon ten thousand Scots died on the battlefield.'

'Ten thousand! How many Romans died?'

'About three hundred. But when the Romans went looking for the survivors the next morning they couldn't find them. They disappeared into the hills, so the Romans could never claim that they'd completely conquered us.'

'This is proper history. How come you know this and I don't?'

Tor looked self-conscious. 'Dunno, might have asked Rhona for more facts, it's no biggie.'

Eder grinned at him. 'There's no shame in being well informed. Nothing embarrassing about being educated.' She paused for a second and then carried on. 'Talking of Romans . . . you know they used to use pigs to fight.'

'No way!' Tor looked excitedly at his sister. 'Like charging war pigs? No, no, wait – I bet they used them for really difficult and dangerous missions. Sneak attacks in the dead of night.'

Eder looked grim. 'Bit nastier than that. They used to cover pigs in oil and tar and then set fire to them. The pigs were so scared they'd squeal and run away, which happened to be towards the enemy. Apparently the squealing was so high-pitched and painful it really upset the enemy elephants.'

Tor looked horrified. 'Like you when you're talking to Taylor.'

Eder nodded in agreement. 'Or you when it's acorn season. Although thinking about it, sometimes you're so excited you can barely breathe, let alone make a noise.'

They sat in silence and watched the sun fall behind

the mountain, a cooling breeze blowing as it slowly disappeared and the land was bathed in darkness. Then they headed back to the farm.

'Who are we going to tell?' asked Eder.

'Why don't we just go?' replied Tor.

'Because they'll worry if we just go missing.'

Tor sighed. 'Fair. Mum?'

'She'd just try and stop us. Anyway, she's still asleep. Rhona?' suggested Eder.

'Too old. She'll give us like loads of advice and lessons on how to cross the road and stuff, and we've got you already so that's the last thing we need. What 'bout Taylor?'

'She sleeps next to Izzy. Too risky. Remember, if Alastair wakes up we may not get out of here at all!'

They both looked at each other. 'Kirstie.'

They found Kirstie sitting outside looking very worried. She was walking round and round a tree in the moonlight and kept flapping her wings as she did so.

'Kirstie!' hissed Eder.

The chicken ignored them and kept walking and flapping.

'Kirstie!'

This time the chicken put her wings over her head to block out the noise.

Tor went and stood on the other side of the tree so that when she rounded it she bumped straight into him. 'What are you doing?' he asked.

'Och, please don't disturb me. I'm still trying to do the homework.'

'What homework? What are you talking about?'

The chicken looked at them in horror. 'The homework your ma set us. Three ways to find north? I can dae it by using the north star at night, and during the day you can see the moss on the trees. I just need a third.' She paused for a second. 'Have you two done it? Have you got three ways? Only, I don't want to copy you.'

Tor just laughed. 'You're kidding?'

'No. I'm not! Mrs Heather'll be so disappointed if

I've nae done it. And it was my first lesson with her, so she'll think I'm lazy!'

Eder was more used to Kirstie so she just nodded. 'Yes, we've done it but I won't tell you what methods we're using because then nobody can accuse you of copying.'

The chicken clucked happily. 'Thanks, Eder, you're a real pal.' She leant over and whispered, 'I don't suppose you did the moth method, did you?'

Eder shook her head. The chicken looked relieved. 'You see, Taylor told me that moths navigate by using the moon's magnetic field. She reckons that if you watch moths by moonlight for long enough you can work out how they do it. So I'm watching them. I'm not going to bed until I've cracked it. I've been here since sunset.' She nodded earnestly.

Tor burst out laughing. 'Taylor told you that? And you believed her? Nice one!'

Kirstie looked confused.

Tor shook his head and carried on, 'Listen, Eder and I are leaving the farm tonight. We're going to look for my father. We need you to tell the others when they wake up so they don't worry. Okay?'

The chicken looked at him in alarm. 'What about school?'

'Did you hear me?' said Tor, speaking very slowly. 'We're leaving the farm. Going away. We may not come back for ages! We need you to tell the others.'

Kirstie nodded. 'Aye, I get that. It's nae bother. You may have to repeat the year though. That's a lot of work. Have you thought this through?'

Tor gave up in despair, but Eder finally managed to convince Kirstie to do what they asked and they set off.

But they'd barely got out of the gate when Joey appeared, his tongue hanging out and panting.

'Kirstie said you were leaving. Where are we going?'

'*We* are going to look for our dad. *You* are staying here.'

The little puppy grinned at them. 'Don't be silly! I'm coming with you.'

Tor looked guilty. 'Not this time, mate. This one we've got to do just the two of us.'

'Yeah. You and me! Adventure pigs together!'

'Me and Eder. I'm afraid this is pigs only, and you're not a pig.'

'Not yet. But I'm going to be when I grow up. Definitely. Pigs are awesome!'

Tor sighed. 'No. Me and Eder are going alone.'

'He means Eder and I,' added Eder helpfully.

'But why can't I come?' said the puppy, looking at them with big brown eyes. 'I don't understand.'

Tor was feeling terrible. 'It's a long way. I don't know when we'll be back. It's not fair to take you.'

'But I want to come. Like you've always said, this farm's too small. I want to see the world with you.'

'But you're not a pig, you're a puppy.'

'I can change! Listen, I've been practising.' The puppy took a deep breath and concentrated really hard. 'Grr-oink! See, I can nearly do it!'

'You'll get tired.'

'I won't! I promise! I'll be really good. Please!!!'

Tor sighed. 'It's not safe. I don't want you to get hurt.'

'I can look after myself! And you need a really good sniffer to find the way. That's me!'

Tor bent down and whispered to the little dog, 'It's actually Eder. She doesn't think you should come.'

'Eder? Why don't you want me?' asked the puppy pathetically.

'Oi! Don't blame me,' said Eder, snorting crossly at her brother. 'It was you who said we shouldn't tell him.'

The puppy looked devastated, like he'd been punched. 'Is that true? Why not? Don't you love me any more?'

Tor took a deep breath, crossed his trotters and lied. 'No, I don't.'

The puppy's lip was quivering as he panted, his tongue hanging out and making him look even younger than usual. Then his eyes narrowed. 'I don't believe you. You're just scared of Dad. Well, I'm *not*. And if you don't take me with you I'm going to bark and bark and wake the entire farm.'

So it was the three of them who set off, the two pigs trotting along and the puppy racing ahead of them, his tail wagging as he tore up and down the road.

'Which way now?' asked Joey when they came to a fork in the road.

Eder went straight across, wriggled through the wire which ran around the field and carried on. 'This way.'

'How do you know?' asked Joey, leaping around them both in a frenzy.

'Because Bennachie is behind us. The Romans came north, and we want to go south, so it makes sense that we go away from Bennachie.'

Joey raced ahead of them and Tor turned to Eder. 'Seriously though, where *are* we going? Where do we start?'

'Mum said she left Dad underground by a town called Gateshead. She also said there was a big angel on a hill.'

'A real angel?'

'No, doofus. A statue.'

'I knew that.'

They walked all through the next night and all the next day before they finally stopped for a rest. It was one of those autumn weeks where the sun seems to be making up for a rubbish summer and is shining away like crazy, and the three travellers tried to spend as much time in streams and water as they could.

It was the apple season, so there was enough to eat, and the chestnuts and acorns would be coming soon. They were making good progress, but despite that, Eder had a sort of niggling feeling. When they settled down that night she waited until Joey was fast asleep and then she went over to Tor.

'Do you think we're doing the right thing?'

'What do you mean?'

'I mean this. Whatever this is.'

'Looking for Aitor?'

'Yes. You don't think we're being stupid?'

'Maybe. Maybe we won't find him, but what's the harm in looking?'

'What if it's a waste of time?'

Tor looked at her. 'Did you have loads of other urgent things to do?'

'You know what I mean.'

'It's an adventure. Enjoy it. Life is nothing more than a series of experiences lived.'

'That's a bit profound for a pig who normally struggles to spell "sty".'

Tor ignored that. His stomach groaned loudly. Eder laughed.

'Dodgy apples,' muttered Tor.

'How many did you have?'

'Only four, but they weren't very ripe. I wish it would hurry up and be acorn season.'

Eder grinned at him. 'Mum always said the apple doesn't fall far from the tree.'

'What does that mean anyway?'

'That you're like Dad. Apparently he loved acorns. Used to drive Mum mad explaining to her how delicious they were. How some varieties were bitter, some were sweet and so on. That's why we're called Ezkurra – it's something like the Basque word for acorn.'

'I know. It's still a stupid name.'

At that point Joey reappeared. His tongue was hanging out and he looked exhausted. He looked at them both expectantly. 'Are we nearly there?'

Chapter 5

Sea-pig!

The next day the puppy and the piglets arrived at their first problem. In front of them was a wide, fast-flowing river. Standing in the middle of it was a man holding a fishing rod and wearing welly boots which came up to his waist.

'We'll have to go further downstream and cross where nobody can see us,' whispered Eder to Tor.

'Why?'

'That man might report us.'

'Who to?'

'The farmer.'

'Who doesn't own us, so won't care. We're pigs. Nobody's looking for us. Why would anyone care if we swim across a river?'

'He will, if we scare away his fish,' argued Eder. 'I don't like it here. I vote we go downstream.'

Tor shook his head. 'I bet it gets even rougher further down. I say we cross here. You're out-voted.'

'How?'

'By me and Joey. Two against one. Right, Joey?'

The puppy barked his agreement loudly and the man in the middle of the stream got such a shock he dropped his rod, lost his balance, wobbled, and then finally sat down in the middle of the river with only his head sticking out of the water. When he stood up again he was furious and waded off down the stream after his rod, shaking an angry fist at the laughing pigs.

Even Eder had to smile as her brother bowed

triumphantly and the man disappeared. 'Problem solved. Hop on, Joey,' said Tor smugly. The puppy jumped onto his back and they started to walk into the river.

Tor had only put one foot in when Joey yelped and jumped off. 'I can't! I'm scared!' said the puppy, looking at the water in horror.

'What of?' asked Tor gently.

The puppy's eyes were wide with fear, his nose quivering wetly as he looked at the river. 'Th-th-that . . .'

Tor sat down next to him. 'I think it's time for your first swimming lesson. We'll start, appropriately enough, with doggy paddle.'

'Just don't make me go in the water.'

As Eder watched, Tor lay down next to Joey, rolled them both so they were on their backs, and then made the puppy bicycle his legs in the air.

'It's basically exactly the same as running, but you do it in the water. The water can't hurt you, as long as you're not scared of it. If you get scared, you panic and then you're in trouble. So, don't panic. I promise you it's fine. It's nothing like the quarry.'

Together they stood in the shallows and then he got Joey to put his head underwater so he could get used to it. Then they lay down and paddled. Finally Tor stood in front of Joey and slowly walked backwards, trying to encourage the puppy to walk towards him. It was going fine until the river bed shelved and Joey was out of his depth. He panicked, paddled frantically, then froze and sank. Tor ducked under and pushed him back into his depth, and the puppy fled up onto the bank in terror.

'You said it wouldn't hurt me! You said I'd float!' wailed the puppy.

'You will,' urged Tor, as Eder nodded in agreement. 'I promise you'll be fine – you just need not to panic and to keep paddling. We need to cross this river.'

'I can't!'

'I thought you wanted to be a pig?' asked Tor innocently. 'Only, pigs love swimming. Don't they, Edds?'

'They love it,' agreed his sister, nodding her head.

The puppy looked so unhappy the pigs took pity on him.

'Can't you carry him across on your back?' asked Eder.

Tor shook his head. 'He's too wriggly. Maybe we could float him across on something?'

They looked for a branch and eventually found one that was big enough that the puppy could almost sit on it completely.

'We'll be either side of you, so all you have to do is keep your eyes shut and hold onto the branch. Adventure pigs, yeah? We'll be over in no time at all.'

Joey nodded bravely and clambered onto the branch. Tor and Eder took one end each and gingerly they eased into the water and set out across the river. Everything was going swimmingly, and the three of them were nearly halfway across, when Eder's eyes shot open and she frantically started mouthing something at Tor. He couldn't understand what she was saying and the more she mouthed it, the more he mouthed, 'What? What?'

Finally Eder could bear it no more and yelped in terror, 'Behind you. Shark!!!!!'

Both Tor and Joey looked round and, sure enough,

there was a massive curved fin slicing through the water towards them at terrifying speed.

Tor yelped in horror and was rewarded with a mouthful of water. Joey howled and then scrabbled and fell off the branch into the river. The three of them were flailing as Joey went under and Tor tried to get hold of him while still staying afloat, but the branch was in the way, and Eder was yelping and then the shark was on them!

They felt themselves dragged down as the shape whooshed under them, and then the shark's head came up underneath all three of them and threw them bodily across the river onto the opposite bank.

They landed and turned to see a huge grey figure leap up out of the water, bark and whoop with delight, and then flip over onto his back as he plunged into the water again with a massive splash. As Joey struggled to get his breath back and Eder shook herself to get some of the water off, a laughing grey head appeared from out of the water, his eyes twinkling, and his funny pointy nose quivering with delight.

'You're not a shark,' said Tor, his legs still quivering with shock.

'No,' whooped the grey creature, laughing and barking. 'I'm a dolphin. Jessie to my friends. I look a tiny bit like a shark because we've both got fins on our backs, but I'm way cleverer and a lot more friendly. Plus, sharks are fish and I'm a mammal.'

'You've got a weird nose,' said Joey as he looked down at the creature.

The dolphin made a grumpy clicking noise. 'Who are you calling weird, four legs? My nose is not weird, it just tapers. Helps me swim. A skill, I could point out, it might benefit you to acquire.'

'Can swim, actually,' replied Joey, who was feeling more confident now he was on dry land.

The dolphin raised his nose. '*Res ipsa loquitur.*'

Even Eder looked puzzled at that one. The dolphin clicked again. 'Why is nobody taught Latin any more? *Res ipsa loquitur* means literally, the thing speaks for itself, i.e. you lot are in the water and you start to sink, thereby proving you can't swim.'

'Are you a Bottlenose?' asked Eder.

The dolphin nodded happily. 'Certainly am. *Tursiops Truncatus*, or Bottlenose dolphin. Actually, it's because of my uniquely tapering nose that some people call me a mereswine, or sea-pig.'

Tor grinned. 'Sea-pig, I like it.'

Eder looked sceptical. 'You're a saltwater dolphin. What are you doing in a river?'

'Fishing,' replied the dolphin. 'I fancied some salmon so thought I'd come upstream. I can swim in either salt or fresh water, but fresh water is a bit tiring, so I usually stay at sea.'

'Someone told me that you are one of the most intelligent creatures of all. That when you sleep only half your brain is actually asleep.'

'What's the other half doing?' asked Tor.

'Thinking,' replied the dolphin. 'It means I'm clever all the time, rather than just when I'm awake.'

'If you're so clever, right,' asked Joey, cockiness now fully restored, 'what's a million hundred million times a million?'

'A million million hundred million,' replied the dolphin.

'Woah!' Joey was impressed. 'That's awesome. Can you . . . um, do you' - he was desperately searching for a really hard question - 'do you know, do you know . . . what's Q in the apple alphabet?'

The dolphin looked thoughtful. 'Apples aren't really my speciality, but I would guess . . . maybe . . . *Queen Cox?*'

Joey looked at Eder for confirmation.

She grinned and nodded. 'He's right. *Q is for Queen Cox, ever so easy to grow, R's the Ribston Pippin, with flesh like sweetened snow.*' Eder looked thoughtful. She turned back to their new friend. 'We're trying to find my father who went missing two years ago in a mine outside a town called Gateshead.'

The dolphin looked at them both. 'So if he's your father he must be either a wild boar or a Duroc?'

'Actually, he's a Bearded pig,' answered Eder. 'From Sumatra. Our mother is a Duroc.'

'Forgive me. Both Bearded piglets and wild boar piglets have stripes, so I assumed you were a wild boar piglet as they are indigenous to Scotland. I also hadn't noticed your beard.'

Tor couldn't resist. 'Yeah, it's a little hard to actually see. Sort of short and tufty.'

Eder looked at him crossly. 'Tor, why don't you explain to Joey what indigenous means?'

Tor grinned. 'No idea, Tufty.' He turned back to the dolphin. 'So, how far are we from Gateshead?'

'Gateshead? That's in England. *Terra incognita* to me, I'm *indigenous* to Scotland I'm afraid.'

He grinned at Eder who smiled back and nodded her head towards her brother.

'Tell him?'

'Indigenous means native, or occurring in one particular place. So I'm from Scotland. If you want to find Gateshead you'll have to cross the Wall.'

'What wall?' asked Eder.

'He means Hadrian's Wall,' answered Tor, keen to get his own back on his sister. 'You remember, I told you about that battle in Scotland, with the Romans? About thirty years after that, the Emperor Hadrian decided he wanted to mark the edge of the Roman empire, so he built a huge wall running across the north of England. He said it would "keep the savages out".'

Eder turned back to the dolphin. 'So what's it like on the other side?'

'No idea. I've never been south of Holy Island. But I'm told it's very like here. Despite what Hadrian said, there is no proof the Scots are any more or less savage than the English.'

'Have you heard of our dad? His name is Aitor Ezkurra.'

The dolphin shook his head. 'I'm afraid not, but then I wouldn't. I don't know much about what happens on land. You should ask someone once you get over the Wall. Just be careful of the Seneschal.'

'Who's that?'

'The Seneschal. Nobody's quite sure what or who he is, but everyone's scared of him. He lives just beyond the Wall and he seems to control all the land around there.'

'Human?' asked Tor.

The dolphin shook his head. 'Apparently he's a wild animal, but nobody has ever seen him, so we can't be sure. Some say he's a badger, others say a lynx, but the most common theory is that he's a grey wolf.'

Eder gulped. 'There are no wolves left – they're extinct.'

The dolphin nodded grimly. 'In Scotland maybe. But Hadrian's Wall is in England, and that's another country. There's wolves, there's packs of wild boars roaming all over the place. It's different down there.'

'So how do we avoid him?'

The dolphin shrugged. 'Don't cross the Wall?'

Joey bared his teeth and tried to look fierce. 'I'll bite him!'

The others ignored that. 'What if we have to?' asked Tor.

'Then, good luck.'

And with a flick of his powerful tail, the dolphin was gone, the ripples in the river the only trace remaining.

Eder turned to Tor. 'Should we turn back? It doesn't sound very safe.'

'You can't duck out on me now. Can I just remind you that this whole "find Dad" thing was your idea?'

'Yeah, I know, but it's just that it sounds a bit scary – I mean, for Joey, obviously. Of course, I'm fine,' she added hastily. She looked over at the little puppy, who was now curled up and dozing on the riverbank.

Tor looked at Eder. 'You can go back if you want, and you'll be okay. You'll spend your life on the farm, and you'll probably end up knowing a load about pears, but nothing about the world. You'll be safe, maybe even pretty happy, but I think there's a part of you that will always wonder. A little nagging voice at the back of your head that thinks: *What if I'd gone on? What if I'd crossed the Wall?*' He grinned at her. 'Ask yourself this – what would Mum do?'

Eder sighed. 'So, this Wall? How far away is it? Is there a stile we can use to climb over?'

'Most of it is ruined now,' replied Tor sadly. Then he perked up. 'I've always wanted to see it. The Romans had a thing about walls – they used to build them all over the place. When it was built, Hadrian's Wall was seventy-three miles long. There are forts every Roman mile, which is the distance a legion can walk in two thousand steps. Come on, let's go.'

Eder pointed to where Joey was lying in a heap, now fast asleep. 'Better wake up the midget.'

'No, we've got a long way to go and he needs his sleep. Can you put him on my back?'

Eder picked up the sleeping puppy and placed him gently across Tor's shoulders. They turned their back on the river and headed south.

Chapter 6

Yew Cannot be Serious . . .

Eder couldn't sleep. She looked over to her brother, breathing deeply with Joey spread-eagled across him. She was thinking about her mum. It was a weird feeling not being with her, especially knowing how ill she was. But something else was nagging at her. Her brother had often talked about the farm being too small, not giving them what they needed.

Something else was missing. She'd thought it was her dad – that was in part why she'd agreed to come on this bonkers adventure with her snoring brother, but it wasn't that either. Not really.

She got up and went for a walk. It felt like they'd been on the road for ages, although as they didn't know where they were supposed to find their dad, it was a bit hard to know how much of the journey they'd completed. They'd stopped to sleep in a wood on the outskirts of a village, and Eder slowly approached the moon-drenched graveyard that marked the edge of the village. She'd always loved graveyards – their quiet calm, the old, old stones, and the history, quite literally under her feet.

The night was crisp and clear, a classic late autumn evening, and in the distance an owl hooted thoughtfully. Eder looked towards the sound and saw something rather odd. Up in the air, just the other side of the graveyard, was a light. Not a bright light, not like a star, no, this was more of a warm greenish glow, as if a candle had been lit inside a balloon. It wasn't scary, and Eder felt drawn towards it.

She trotted over, taking care not to tread on any graves, and realised it was actually slightly further than she'd thought. She left the graveyard and ventured a little way towards the village, taking care not to make any noise, or to risk tripping over anything.

The glow was coming from inside a sort of enclosure with railings around it. Anything with a railing around it and a padlock on the gate is usually two things: one, forbidden to piglets; and two, very interesting. Eder squeezed through the railings to see what was inside.

It was a tree. A yew, if Eder wasn't mistaken. But as she walked around the edge of it she realised that this was bigger than any yew tree she'd ever seen. Bigger in fact than any tree of any sort. It was huge. It must have been sixteen metres around, although because it was sort of hollow in the middle it looked like two flat trees facing each other. The wood was gnarled and knotty, with all the branches bent, wizened and twisted, almost as though they'd been deformed by years and years of holding up the leaves, branches and fruits of the tree above. How old must it be?

Eder sniffed at it and the smell of yew filled her snout and then drifted out again, leaving behind it a sense of old age, solidity and history.

The glow was coming from the branches above the middle, so Eder peered cautiously into the middle of the tree before putting her front trotters inside to get a closer look. It was strange, and almost magical, as the two trunks had obviously once been opposite sides of one vast trunk, but over the years much of the middle of the tree had either died or been removed, so now it was almost like a hollow shell. Still very much alive though, and as Eder clambered completely inside, she could almost feel as though she were stepping into the past.

It was only now, once she was sort of inside the tree that she could really grasp its full size. It towered above her and around her, and she felt as if she was standing in the middle of a great wood fountain, bursting out of the earth and exploding like a bomb, its leaves and foliage flattening out into a mushroom cloud of green. She gazed upwards in awe to where she could see the glow, clearly visible now, about two metres up in the tree, the foliage around too thick for her to see it clearly, but it was there nonetheless. Surprisingly, she wasn't scared at all now – she was just desperate to know what it was.

Resting her front trotters on a branch, she experimentally hopped up. That was okay. She made it onto the first branch and then looked for a second. She managed that too, but then started to run into trouble. Pigs weren't built for climbing trees, even trees as gnarled and branchy as this one. She cast around for somewhere to stand but it seemed hopeless.

'Need a hand?' The voice came from out of the middle of the glow!

Eder panicked, lost her footing and one trotter slid off the branch. She flailed, wobbled, and was about to plummet down to the ground when she felt a hand steadying her.

'That's better. Here, let me help you. Come on, if you put one trotter there, then we can move the other ones over here and then I'll give you a little heave and, whoops, there we go, you're there.'

Eder found herself pushed up through a layer of leaves to a flat bit higher up in the tree. The branches criss-crossed and made a sort of platform where she could rest. There was the glow, and a shadowy figure, sort of half lit. What was it?

'It's a Kindle. An electronic book. It's really my dad's, but he's said I can use it,' said the voice, almost as if it could read Eder's thoughts. A hand picked it up and held it out towards Eder. It was a sort of flat thing with light coming out of it and words written on it. Weird book. How would Rhona be able to read that? The hand turned the book around and shone the light on Eder, and a boy looked closer and then gasped with delight.

'A Bearded pig! That's awesome! I thought you were a boar piglet, but I hadn't seen the beard. Could I?' The boy tentatively reached out, and Eder allowed him to gently stroke her beard. 'Bearded pigs are the *best*. Dad took me to see them in London Zoo but that was years ago! I didn't think there were any in Scotland, certainly no piglets. Are you one of the ones who broke out of the zoo? You can't be, as that was over two years ago. This is so cool. Are you hungry?'

At the very moment he said that, Eder's stomach growled and the boy grinned at her. 'Thought so. Here.' He reached into his pocket and fished out a pear. 'It's a pear, so I hope that's okay? I'm Finn, by the way.'

Eder snuffled happily and the boy grinned again as he took a bite and then passed it to the peckish piglet. She hadn't realised how hungry she was and she happily wolfed it down. She knew this one. It was a *Comice, a dumpy pear, lychee-sweet with juicy flesh but a tough greeny-brown skin.*

'I couldn't sleep so I came here to read in the tree. I love it here. It's my best thinking place. Nobody's supposed to climb this tree because it's so old. More than three thousand years old, in fact. It's the oldest living thing in Britain. Maybe in the world. Did you know yew trees are the only living creature biologically capable of living indefinitely? Their branches grow down to the ground and they form other trunks which are really the same tree. And when one trunk dies, another grows inside it. And this is the oldest one of all. It's right in the middle of Scotland, the natural heart of the whole country. Dad says there's magic running through it and that's why there's a fence around it. To stop people hurting it any more. Druids used to take bits of it and use it in their spells.'

Finn paused for a second and pointed upwards through the leaves of the tree to where they could see the stars glittering and sparkling up in the night sky. 'Christmas trees started because apparently someone was walking in a forest and saw the stars twinkling through the leaves of the tree. He thought it would be wicked to decorate a tree like that. But they used to only do it with one branch. A big branch, but only a branch. They'd hang presents off it and stuff. Then one year Queen Charlotte had so many presents to give she decided she needed something bigger. So she got her gardeners to dig up a whole yew tree and put it right in the middle of the palace drawing room with toys and sweets all over it. When all the children came in they thought it was magic and that the tree had grown up through the floor.' Finn leant closer to Eder and dropped his voice. 'Sometimes, when I lie really still and listen as hard as I can, I can hear whispering. I don't know what it's saying, as it's probably speaking in tree, but I can definitely hear it talking.'

Finn and Eder lay side by side on their backs in the tree and listened as hard as they could, but neither of them heard anything.

'Hello . . . tree,' said Finn in a serious voice. Then, '*Hello, little human and four-footed animal,*' he answered himself in a deep tree-like voice. '*Do you seek my counsel?*'

Eder snuffled happily as she listened to Finn being silly.

'We seek to know the future. We want to know what will become of Finn and his new friend, the Bearded piglet. Can you tell us, o mighty tree?' . . . '*I cannot predict the future, little human, but I will tell you that this pig is true and loyal, and will never let you down.*'

Eder rolled over and tried to see what her new

friend looked like. It was still very dark though, so she couldn't really make him out. Then, almost as if he'd been reading her mind again, Finn spoke.

'You're probably wondering who I am?' He turned the funny book round again and shone the light on his face. It showed a young boy of about eleven or twelve years old, lightly freckled and skinny, with hair that stuck up like candles on a birthday cake. 'My full name is Finlay MacGregor, but everyone calls me Finn. I'm twelve. Nearly. I live in a hotel because my mum's the cook so we live there.' His hand pointed off into the darkness somewhere. 'My dad builds roads so he's away loads. He's building a road in Skye at the moment. That's an island north of here. He's not here because roads take a really long time to build, but he says the thing about building a road is that you never get lost. You just follow the road back to where you started. He'll be home soon. You'll really like him. What's your name?' Finn stared at Eder as if he really expected her to answer.

She oinked 'Eder' at him hopefully, but obviously he couldn't understand her.

'Don't have one, eh? Let's ask the tree.' He cleared his throat. 'Wise and ancient yew tree, who has been here for many years and is responsible for me meeting this new friend, can you tell me what name you bestow upon this magnificent Bearded piglet?'

There was silence, and then Finn bent down and pressed his head to the tree. He nodded as the tree whispered to him. Then he sat up again.

'The tree says your name is Iona. After the island of Iona, which was once called Yew Tree Island.'

Eder turned her new name over and over inside her head. Iona, Iona, Iona. It sounded like a breath of air, a sort of contented sigh. It was a good name. She was pleased.

Finn rolled over so he was completely on Eder's level. He put the Kindle down between them so they were both lit from underneath, which made them look spooky and a bit scary. 'So, Iona pig, you don't say much, do you? I bet you can understand me though – Bearded pigs are really clever. Let's do an experiment. If you understand what I'm saying, then scrunch your snout.'

Eder nearly fell out of the tree. He was Isla! But a boy. She scrunched her snout vigorously and was rewarded with a loud 'hah!' from Finn.

'I knew it!' he added happily. 'This is excellent. I'm in my favourite place in the whole world, reading a book and thinking I'd really like a chat, and who should appear but a Bearded pig? The most intelligent and handsome of all pigs. Man, I love this tree!'

Eder wasn't quite sure what it had to do with the tree, but she knew one thing – she liked this boy. She wanted him to keep talking to her. She wanted him to be her boy. She shuffled forward and shyly pushed her snout into his hand.

The next thing Eder knew was when she woke up to find the sun was coming over the horizon and they were both covered in dew. Tor! Joey! She had to get back. She jumped to her feet and then oinked in panic as she remembered she was actually halfway up a tree! Her oink woke Finn, who also sat up in alarm.

'Oh no! What time is it? I've got to go. Dad might be back! And Mum hates it if I'm not there when she wakes up.' He scrambled down the tree and then stood underneath and looked up. 'Iona, jump! I'll catch you,' he called up.

Eder was scared. There was no way – it was too far down.

Finn held out his arms. 'Come on, Iona, jump!'

But she just couldn't.

Finn clambered back up the tree, wedged his foot in one of the branches and lifted Eder onto his shoulders, wrapping her trotters around his neck. Very gently and gradually he took his foot out and stepped down to find a foothold lower down the trunk. Clinging on with his arms, he gradually slid down, and little by little they reached the ground.

They walked over to the gate together, both knowing they had to part, but neither wanting to. Eder slid through the railings and Finn clambered over the wall. They looked at each other a bit awkwardly, neither one of them wanting to be the first to go.

'I had fun last night,' said Finn as he sat on his haunches in front of Eder.

Me too, me too! thought Eder loudly, her legs jiggling frantically as she tried to convey her agreeing to him.

'I'm sure you can understand me,' said Finn. 'I've never been so sure of anything, ever.'

I do understand you! I do! I can! thought Eder as hard as she could. She oinked frantically and scrunched her snout vigorously to try and make him understand.

Finn looked at her sideways, as if he were puzzling over something. He put his hand down and stroked her. Then he did a really weird thing. He reached up to his cheek, and pinched himself really hard. 'Ow!!!' he yelped, his cheek turning red as he did. Then he grinned. 'You're still here! I had a horrible feeling I might have dreamed the whole thing. Listen, I've got to go or I'll be late for school, but will you chum me after? I've got pipe band practice and then I've got loads of homework, but I'll meet you here after that? Scrunch if that's a plan.'

Eder scrunched.

Finn grinned at her, saluted her with one finger and then ran off into the mist.

Seconds later he ran back.

'I've got a riddle for you. You'll never get it, but think about it while I'm gone and I'll tell you the answer later.' He looked into Eder's eyes and put on his 'tree voice' again. *'What word becomes shorter when you add two letters to it?'*

Chapter 7

I Can't Stand
the Rain!

Joey was just waking up when Eder got back. She'd found a couple of early-season conkers which she offered the sleepy puppy for his breakfast. He wasn't keen though, so she and Tor shared them while Joey dashed off to get some apples he'd spotted the day before.

Tor yawned and stretched. 'Sleep well, sis?'

'Uh huh.' Eder couldn't quite meet his eye. She pushed the conkers towards him and Tor yawned and tucked in.

'I've been thinking about where we go. You see, what I've been reckoning is that from what Mum says, Dad would have definitely tried to come and find us, yes?'

Eder nodded, her mouth full of conker.

'So as he hasn't,' Tor continued, 'something must have stopped him. Yes?'

'Fair enough,' agreed Eder. 'So what could that have been? He got held up?'

'For two years?'

'Lost?'

'Maybe, but Mum reckons he was pretty good at navigating, and they managed to get all the way up from the south of England before they got separated, so I'm not thinking that's very likely.'

'Agreed, so what then?' asked Eder.

'I don't know. Isn't this the bit where you're all brainy and suggest a solution?'

'It's a democracy. I don't want to impose my decisions on the group.'

'You force away, I'm all ears.'

Eder shook her head. 'No, because then, in years to come, you'll just say I bullied you.'

Tor burst out laughing. 'You? Bullied me? Really?'

Eder tutted.

Tor stood up. 'I say we go to Hadrian's Wall, and then we decide when we get there,' he said. 'It can't be much further. If we set off as soon as Joey gets back we'll be there in a day or two.'

Eder panicked. 'No!'

'Sorry?'

'We can't go! We've got to stay here.'

Tor looked puzzled. 'Why? I thought you were in a rush.'

Eder's heart was racing. She could never lie to her brother as he always saw straight through her. 'I am. I mean, we are. But we've got to stay here. Because . . . it's raining!'

'Eder, it's late October in Scotland. Of course it's raining.'

'But we'll get wet.'

'We're pigs. Getting wet is what we do.'

'But I don't like it. I never have. We should stay here. Where it's dry. What word becomes shorter when you add two letters?'

'What?'

'You heard me. It's a riddle.'

'I have no idea. Why are you trying to change the subject?'

Fortunately for Eder, at that moment the rain really started coming down, and seconds later Joey appeared through it, dripping wet. He shook himself vigorously all over the piglets. Then he dropped the thing he'd been carrying, lay down and started to eat it. It was an entire cabbage.

'Where on earth did you find a cabbage?' asked Tor as he rolled on the ground to get dry.

'Gmma rrrmdmy!' answered the piglet.

'Don't talk with your mouth full,' said Tor reproachfully.

'Sorry, Dad!' grinned the puppy as he swallowed.

The trio stayed where they were all day, sheltering from the rain in an old disused hut. By the time it finally stopped, the moon was out and it was too late to really make a start.

Eder waited until the other two were fast asleep before getting up and sneaking out. She ran as fast as she could to the tree, but there was nobody there. Hoping she was just not seeing properly she trotted right round the tree, oinking quietly, but there was no reply. It was strange – she'd only known this boy for one day, but she felt really sad that he wasn't there. She walked into the middle of the tree, where it was all hollowed out, and lay down, feeling utterly miserable.

She must have fallen asleep because she started having the strangest dream she'd ever had. In it, she was running down a hill being chased by giant onions and Brussels sprouts which were rolling after her like huge cannonballs, threatening to squash her. She woke up with a start and there, right in front of her, was a massive onion! Eder jumped up in horror, oinking in panic, and then saw Finn's anxious face looking at her in alarm.

'Iona, are you okay?' he asked, and he sounded so worried, and Eder was so pleased to see him, that her heart did a little skip, and she jumped at him, knocking him backwards and nuzzling him as she landed on top of him.

Finn was laughing as Eder rolled off him and tickled his nose, making him beg her to stop before he sneezed.

Tor was fast asleep when he felt a little figure snuggling up to him. He groaned and tried to force his eyes open. It was Joey. The puppy wasn't really awake, but he felt hot and a bit shivery.

'Are you okay? Bad dream?' asked Tor sleepily.

'The river . . .' nodded the little puppy as he inched closer, and within seconds his eyes were closed and he was breathing deeply again.

Tor tried to get back to sleep again but it was no use. He couldn't really move because Joey was squashed up against him, and every time he tried to move the puppy just snuggled even closer. He lay there thinking and suddenly something struck him.

He whispered, 'Eder!' There was no reply. He tried again, a bit louder. 'EDER!' But still nothing. He stickily slipped out of Joey's sweaty embrace and went over to the pile of leaves where Eder slept. It was empty. What's more, when he felt the leaves, they were cold. She hadn't been in them for a while.

Tor looked around but the ground was hard and he couldn't immediately see where she might have gone. He looked at Joey, fast asleep now, and wondered if he could leave him? He wouldn't be gone long, just to have a quick scout around. Where on earth was Eder?

He set off but had only gone a few paces when he turned back. He couldn't leave the puppy alone. Instead, he went back and nudged Joey until he woke up and yawned.

'Is it morning time?' he asked sleepily.

'Not quite, mate, but I need you. How's your nose?'

'Good. Why?'

'Because I need you to track Eder.'

'Where's she gone?'

'That's what we're going to find out. Come on, it's a secret mission.'

The puppy got up excitedly, sniffed at Eder's pile of leaves and then set off, nose to the ground, in the direction of the graveyard. Tor followed behind him.

Eder had finished the onion and was lying on her tummy with her head resting on Finn's lap while he told her about his school and what he'd been up to.

'Actually, this is my favourite time of year. Because the days are short – oh, that was the answer to the riddle. You add the two letters "e" and "r" to the word "short" to get "shorter". Clever, huh? Dad told me that in his last letter. He usually texts me, but he says people don't write letters enough and it's really cool when you get one, so sometimes he writes to me as well. He's always asking me riddles and questions and jokes and he asked me another one too. He said I should solve them both before he comes back, but I can't. Listen, think really hard. "What's stronger than God, more evil than the Devil, the rich want it, the poor have it, and if you eat it you die?" I can't work it out. I asked everyone at school but they can't do it either. I told Mum about you and she thought I was making you up, so will you come and meet her?'

He paused and looked down at Eder. Her head was placed against his chest and she could feel his heart beating. She rolled over onto her back and looked up at his questioning face. How on earth was she going to tell him that tomorrow she had to leave him? Instead, she scrunched.

Finn grinned and jumped up. 'Come on, then! Let's go. She'll still be working so we'll go the long way round. Have you ever seen MacGregor's Leap? It's named after one of my ancestors. Come on, I'll show you.' He climbed out of the tree and headed towards the gate. Eder followed him happily.

'Where's she going? And who's that with her?' asked Joey. Tor and Joey were hidden in a bush, watching Eder and Finn and trying to work out what to do next.

They had been watching her for about five minutes from their hiding place. Joey had been keen to go and say hello but Tor was more cautious. There was something about this situation that was holding him back. It wasn't that he was scared, or even worried, it was more that he could see how happy Eder looked, and that made him happy and sad at the same time. He wondered why she hadn't told him. It did explain her weird behaviour with the rain yesterday though. He grinned to himself as he remembered her flustered objections. He'd known something was up, and now he knew what. He flexed a trotter which had gone to sleep and nudged Joey.

'Come on, mate, I think we should follow her. But be careful. We don't want to scare her, or make her think we're spying on her.'

'But we are spying on her,' said Joey, sounding a bit puzzled.

'Shush. Do as you're told.'

As they followed the boy and the piglet, Tor was thinking. He and Eder always told each other everything. So why hadn't she told him about this boy?

'She must really love him,' said Joey as if he could read Tor's thoughts.

'What do you mean by that?' asked Tor.

'She's eating an acorn. She hates acorns.'

Joey was right. The boy was offering Eder an acorn and she was hoovering it up as if it were a delicious parsnip, or even a tasty *Bartlett* pear.

Eder trotted happily after Finn who was wittering on about his dad and how he was an amazing swimmer. Eder let the words wash over her, as she didn't particularly need to hear what Finn was saying – it was more the sound of his voice she liked. They were walking down a path through a wood. It was dark in the wood, and spongy under her trotters. The moonlight was making some amazing spooky shadows as they walked, and although Eder couldn't feel one, she was sure there was an evening breeze because the bracken was rustling as the wind disturbed it and made it sound almost alive.

'Shhh!!!' hissed Tor to Joey, who was leading the way and managing to make a terrible racket as he brushed through the bracken on either side of the path.

'I'm trying!' whispered Joey. 'But it's not easy. Why can't we walk on the path?'

'Because they mustn't see us! We're on a secret mission, remember? We're spy pigs.'

Eder could hear a strange rumbling, roaring sound which didn't belong in the forest at all. It reminded her more of traffic on a motorway, or of one of the farm machines. She followed Finn as he led her past a tree and the whole world seemed to open out in front of her. She was gazing down at a huge river running right below them, tumbling over the rocks and churning as it rushed past them, uncaring and unaware.

'It's cool, isn't it?' asked Finn as he sat down next to her, his legs dangling over the edge of the bank. 'This is MacGregor's Leap. It's nearly four metres across to the other side.'

Eder looked. It did seem an awfully long way.

Finn continued excitedly, 'It's called that after my

great-great-great grandfather. He was being chased by these dogs – bloodhounds with big teeth – and they'd nearly caught him and he was exhausted so this was his last hope. Nobody had ever made the leap before, because it's so far, and obviously if you don't make it across you end up in the river. But he had no choice, so he jumped from this very spot and he made it to the other side and escaped. Nobody's dared to try it since.'

Eder gulped as she looked across and huddled closer to Finn for safety. And as she did, his phone buzzed. He pulled it out of his pocket and looked at the display.

'Och, it's a text from Ma. What does she want?' He opened it. *Come home now*, he read. He turned to Eder. 'It must be Dad! She's said I'm to come home. He must be back! Come on! Let's go.' He turned and ran back into the woods. Eder raced after him.

Joey was curious to see MacGregor's Leap, so the two of them had a quick look, gulped in alarm, and then Joey put his nose to the ground and set off again. 'Eder has a very distinctive smell,' the puppy commented as he sniffed his way along. 'It's sort of warm – milky, kind of.'

'What does her friend smell of?' asked Tor, not really very interested, as he looked ahead, trying to see where they'd gone.

'Biscuits, sweat, that yew tree, and a strange smell I can't quite place. I've smelt it before but I can't remember when.'

They reached the edge of the wood and saw a large building with cars outside.

Joey nodded towards it. 'That's where they've gone. They're in that building.'

'I wonder what it is?'

'It's a hotel,' answered the puppy.

'How on earth do you know that?'

'There's a big sign. Fort-something hotel.'

'Well, if Eder's inside, we better be as well.'

Chapter 8

Pigs in Blankets . . .

Eder followed Finn as he ran round the hotel to the back. She was having to scamper to keep up with him and he must have realised, because at the back door he stopped and waited for her to catch up.

'This is where I live. In this hotel. Mum works in the kitchens and we live in a room in the basement. Two rooms, because I've got my own one. Not posh guest rooms – they're just like normal bedrooms. You can sleep on the floor tonight. We're not supposed to have any pets indoors so we'll have to be careful.'

Eder scrunched nervously.

The hotel was on the edge of the wood, but there was open space all around it. Lawns on the sides, and in front a big parking area full of cars.

'Okay, here's the plan,' said Tor quietly. 'This is like real live war pigs. We've got to be super quiet and very sneaky. We'll crawl across the car park and hide under the car nearest the door. You can bark really loudly and someone will come out to see what's going on. I'll take that opportunity to dash inside. Once I'm in, then I'll wait until the coast's clear and then I'll nudge the door ajar for you to follow me inside. Got it?'

'Why don't we just use that open window over there?' asked Joey reasonably.

'All right, clever paws, we'll do it your way.'

The two of them slipped quietly and carefully across

the car park to the open window Joey had spotted. There was a bench nearby, and together they shoved it until it was under the window. They scrambled up and looked inside.

The room was full of books in bookcases, and in the middle of it was a large table with a soft-looking green top and coloured balls all over it. Tor got his snout under the bottom of the window and pushed it up until he and Joey could fit through, and then they both jumped down inside.

They looked around the room and saw a door in one corner. It was shut.

'Trotters!' muttered Tor.

Joey giggled as he always did when his big cousin used a bad word. 'What's wrong?' he asked.

'The door's shut and the hinges are on the inside, which means it opens inwards. We're stuck.'

Finn led the way through the door and into the hotel. Just inside was a sort of room full of coats and boots and sticks. Eder was suddenly quite nervous and froze just inside the door. Finn was by her side in an instant. 'Don't be scared,' he said in a reassuring voice. 'We'll be fine. My dad's really friendly and my mum's okay. Just stick close to me.' He paused for a second. 'Would it help if I made you a sort of lead? So we can't be separated? And everyone knows you're with me?'

Eder scrunched, and so Finn fished a big white handkerchief out of his pocket. He found a pen on the table and wrote: *Iona MacGregor, Fortingall Hotel, Aberfeldy, Perthshire* on the hankie. Then he tied a good strong knot in it and secured it loosely around her neck. He grabbed a piece of string, tied one end around the handkerchief and the other end to his wrist.

'Okay? Now everyone knows who you are, and where I live. If you get lost, just give someone that hankie and they'll bring you back here.'

Eder snuffled happily and followed Finn as he headed off into the hotel, the lead in his hand.

'Right. Back to the first plan,' said Tor to Joey as they confronted the closed door. We hide behind the door, you bark like mad, someone comes in and we run out. Once we're outside, follow me and don't stop until I do. Okay?'

'What then?' asked the puppy.

'We find Eder and we get out of here,' replied Tor decisively. 'Ready? One, two, three, *bark*!'

Eder was trotting along behind Finn, trying to take everything in. There was a wooden floor that was so shiny she could see the underneath of her own tummy, huge paintings on the walls, and lots of heavy dark wood furniture. There was a man up a ladder with a long sheet of paper that he was trying to stick to the wall.

'Give us a hand here, Finn lad?' asked the man as they approached him and Finn stepped forward to help.

'This is Iona, she's a Bearded pig friend of mine,'

said Finn as he held the wallpaper tight at the bottom and the man smoothed it from the top. 'You okay now? Only my mum called and told me to come. I think my dad's home. Have you seen him?'

The man laughed and shook his head. 'Go on then, lad, off you go. Thanks for your help.'

Finn and Eder continued down the corridor, round a corner and then down some stairs into the basement. There was a huge container full of sheets and pillows at the bottom of a laundry chute, and next to it was a door which Finn opened to reveal the kitchen.

The noise was amazing. There were people everywhere, banging pans, crashing plates, washing up, cooking things and shouting at each other – so much noise that Eder was terrified. She hid between Finn's legs and he grinned down at her.

'Bit loud, huh? Don't worry, you stay there.' He waved across the room and a nice-looking woman with her hair up under a silly white hat waved back and came over to them. She looked hot and sweaty, not helped by the fact that some hair had escaped from the hat and she was having to blow it off her face. Finn mouthed, 'Dad?' at her as she came, but she shook her head and looked apologetic, and Eder felt Finn slump as the hope drained out of him.

In the billiards room Joey was barking furiously, and Tor was oinking as loudly as he could. They heard noises outside and prepared themselves, so as a man in a uniform opened the door and came in to see what was going on, the two of them shot through his legs and out of the room. They emerged into a long corridor with a shiny polished floor, which seemed to stretch for ages in each direction. Up ahead was a man doing something on a ladder so that way was blocked.

Tor turned round and looked the other way. It was clear, and he and Joey were about to set off when the man in uniform came out of the room where they'd been before and blocked their path.

'What in heaven's name is going on?' he said as he looked at the two animals in amazement. 'A pig and a puppy, in ma hotel! It will nae do.' He started to run towards them and Joey and Tor turned and fled straight towards the man with the ladder.

As they ran, Tor spotted a staircase leading up to the right and he barked, 'That way! Up the stairs,' to the puppy at his side.

Both of them tried to brake and disaster struck. Unable to get any hold on the slippy wooden floor, both dog and piglet skidded, lost any sort of grip and shot with terrifying speed straight past the staircase and right into the bottom of the ladder! The ladder flew sideways, the bucket of glue tipped out all over the animals, and the man was left, halfway up the wall, holding onto the strip of wallpaper for dear life. Sadly it wasn't quite strong enough, and as he scrabbled to hold it in place, the paper peeled off the wall and deposited the man on top of the sticky, wriggling animals.

Finn's mum had led them out of the kitchen into the relative calm of the basement and had her arm round

Finn as she talked to him. She had a lovely gentle voice, but Finn did not want to hear what she was saying to him.

Upstairs Tor was wriggling around in the wallpaper and the glue as the two men tried to grab him. Joey found his feet and slid towards the staircase.

'Come on!' shouted the puppy, and Tor suddenly was on his feet. He skidded over to the staircase and the two of them bolted upstairs. They rounded a corner and ran straight into a chambermaid, who was shaking out sheets and pillowcases in the middle of the upstairs corridor. Behind them they heard the man in uniform coming up the stairs and shouting, 'Grab them!' to the chambermaid.

They were trapped!

Finn was standing opposite his mother and shouting.

His eyes were filling up with tears and his nose was starting to run.

'No, you're wrong. He is coming. He's taking me camping. He's going to show me the road he's building.'

'I'm so sorry, love. It's just the way things are.'

'You said he was coming back! You *promised*!'

'I thought he was, my love.'

'But why! Where is he now? Is he still in Skye? Maybe he hasn't finished the road yet? He'll come back when it's done, won't he? Please?'

Finn's mum took a deep breath. 'I'm afraid not, love. The road's all finished. He's in Glasgow. He wants me to send his stuff to Glasgow.'

'What stuff?'

'You know, his clothes and his books and whatnot.'

'Don't send it! You mustn't. If you don't send it, then he'll have to come home to get it and we can talk to him. I won't go to school and I'll wait for him and we can make him stay. He hasn't even met Iona yet.'

Finn's mum wrapped her arms around him and

buried his head in her shoulder. She was stroking his hair and saying, 'There there' in a soothing voice as he tried not to burst into tears.

He felt a snout pushing into his hand, and a tufty beard stroking his palm. It tickled and he giggled, which made him hiccup and look down at the worried Bearded piglet by his side.

Tor didn't know what to do. He and Joey were stuck. Quite literally, given that he was glued to a sheet with wallpaper paste! Their adventure was over. He poked his head out of the folds of sheet and looked at the chambermaid in despair, his ears flopping over his eyes miserably. She grinned at him, and then, as the man clattered up the stairs, she grabbed a handle on the wall and opened a chute.

'Quick! Down there!' She smiled, picked up the load of sheets and pillows and shoved the lot, including the animals, into the metal chute. As she slammed it shut, and Tor and Joey both slid down the metal tunnel, the last they heard was the uniformed man arriving and panting, 'Where are they?' as their saviour chambermaid innocently replied, 'Who?'

They slid down the chute, getting faster and faster, tumbling over as they went until finally they shot out into the laundry bin just by the kitchen. Joey landed on top of Tor and the piglet had to flail around with his trotters to try and avoid being suffocated. One of the pillows tore and feathers burst out, so the more Tor wriggled, the more they flew in the air and got stuck to him and Joey.

'Tor! What on earth are you two doing here?' It was Eder, jumping up at the side of the laundry bin, trying to see inside. A pair of hands reached in and pulled out the wriggling piglet and the over-excited puppy. The two of them sat on the ground while Finn and his mum looked at them in amazement.

'I don't know what to say,' said Finn.

'Nor do I,' added his mother.

'Where's that pig!!!!' came a shout from upstairs, and there was the sound of a heavy set of footsteps on their way downstairs.

'Eder! He's after us. We've got to go,' yelped a panicked Tor. 'He's been chasing us all round the hotel!'

Eder looked at Finn and scrunched. Once.

He realised she was trying to tell him something and looked at her closely. She tugged at the lead as if to say 'we've got to go' and he grasped it instantly.

'You know these two?'

Eder scrunched.

'The porter is chasing them?'

Eder scrunched.

'They need to go?'

A third scrunch from Eder.

'Come on then!' He turned round and headed towards a door past the kitchen. 'Mum, can you hold him up? Please.' And then he and the three animals went through the door just as the red-faced manager appeared round the corner.

'Ah, Morag, have you seen by any chance a brace of animals come this way? There was a pig, a Duroc boar if I'm not much mistaken, and a wee puppy. He'd a look of a sheepdog about him, but much smaller.'

Finn's mum considered the question. 'Aye, well, funny you should ask that. There was a pig down here not ten minutes ago.' The man's face lifted in hope, then she carried on. 'But he was a Saddleback, not a Duroc.' She shook her head and smiled. 'Of course I haven't seen a pig and a dog, you daft article. This is a hotel, nae a zoo, or am I missing something?'

The man looked rueful and sighed deeply. 'There *was* a pig,' he muttered as he walked away back up the stairs. 'I saw him, and a dog as well. You'll see. I'll find 'em.'

The animals he'd seen were at the back door of the hotel just saying goodbye to Finn. He had removed the sheet from Tor and was now trying to get all the feathers off as well.

'That was amazing! First I meet Iona in my favourite tree – I always said it was magic and that's the proof right there – and then you two as well. Where on earth did you come from? I mean, I know you can't answer, but it's strange. There've been no sightings of pigs here for years, apart from some wild boars, and then you arrive out of the blue. And with a puppy as well. I don't think I can pick off any more of these feathers without hurting you. If my dad were here I could borrow some white spirit, but . . .' He tailed off at the mention of his dad, and Eder snuggled in extra close and stuck her snout into his hand.

'Eder, we should go,' said Tor.

'But . . .' Eder didn't know what to say.

'That man'll be back soon, and we have to go.'

'Will you at least let me say goodbye? Go and wait for me in the woods. I'll be there in a minute.'

Tor and Joey scampered off, leaving Finn and Eder sitting on the steps of the hotel.

Eder turned to look at Finn, her ears flopping over her eyes as she snuggled up to him. Finn turned her snout towards him and flipped back her ears so he could see her eyes properly.

'You going with them?'

There was a long pause and then Eder half-scrunched.

'You don't have to,' said Finn quietly. 'You could stay.'

Eder's head felt like it was going to explode. Did

she have to go? Why? She was on a mad quest to find someone she didn't know, had no real feelings for, and who might not even be alive. It was bonkers. Here was someone she had a connection with. Someone who needed her . . .

Suddenly she knew what she'd been missing. She understood what it was about the farm that didn't make her happy. She wasn't *needed*. Finn needed her. Why not stay? Sadly he untied the lead and took it off, along with the handkerchief collar.

'I'll hang onto this,' he said as he put it into his pocket. 'If you ever need anything, you know where to find me.'

She scrunched at him sadly, and then thrust her snout possessively into his grubby, feather-covered hand.

'Hey, I almost forgot. I got you something.' He rolled her off and sat up, then reached into the pocket of his jacket and handed over an apple. *Spartan, deep-red skin with a pineapple taste and crisp, white flesh.* Most importantly of all, it was Heather's favourite apple, and seeing one there suddenly brought her mother flooding back to Eder. She missed her terribly, just as she would miss Finn if she left. Two people who loved her unconditionally, whatever she did.

She'd already left one of them. Could she bring herself to do it a second time?

Chapter 9

The Wizard in the Wall

They walked for what seemed like weeks without stopping, apart from to grab some sleep, and to eat whatever food they could find. Every animal they passed they asked for news of Aitor, but nobody had heard of him. They thought about giving up, but then they remembered Heather and that gave them the strength to carry on.

Then, just when they were getting really fed up, they reached it. They had been walking up a hill and as Tor reached the top, he looked down and gasped.

'Wow.' He sat down on his haunches and drank in the sight. 'I never thought I'd actually see it.'

'What? What?' barked Joey, who was scrambling up behind him.

'The Wall.'

They were on the very top of a hill, and down in the valley below them, snaking over the hills in front of them was a drystone wall. It twisted and turned, following the curves of the hillside, almost as if it had once been straight, but the hills had shrugged until they got comfortable and now it followed a more random course. The section they were looking at was about three or four stones high, but as you looked along it you could see some places where it had fallen completely, and others where there was little more than a ditch, a mound of earth, or a few stones marking the line.

'Seventy-three miles long, eight feet wide and up to fifteen feet high. It was the largest thing the Romans ever built,' commented an awestruck Tor.

Joey looked at it. Was he missing something? What were the pigs getting so excited about?

'Come on!' shouted Eder excitedly. 'Let's go and see it.'

She and Tor raced down the hill, leaving Joey sitting at the top. As he watched the two of them snuffling about as excitedly as if they were doing an Easter acorn hunt, the puppy was a bit disappointed. All this fuss they'd made, and really? It was just a wall. A few stones piled on top of each other.

Ever since he could remember, he'd longed for one thing – to be a pig, just like his big brother Tor. He wasn't really his brother, or even his cousin of course. He knew that, but it felt like he was. Tor had always been there, always a year or so ahead of Joey, always looking after him, playing with him, knowing the answer in class, inventing a new game about war pigs, just being really cool. Taylor, Joey's big sister, used to laugh at him for secretly practising his 'oink', and swearing that when he grew up he was definitely going to have a curly tail like Tor, maybe even a beard like Eder. It was always *when*, never *if*. But for the last few days, since they'd left the farm, in fact, Joey had to admit that he was starting to wonder if, maybe, he wasn't cut out to be a pig?

It wasn't just that they seemed so interested in food and rolling in the mud, or that they didn't want to run all the time like he did. It was more than that. He didn't know what, but something wasn't there. Something was missing. He set off and scampered down the hill after them.

'So . . . is this really amazing?' asked Joey hesitantly. He was trying extra hard to be interested, and to understand what it was that was so fascinating about this wall. 'So these stones? They're really nice, and sort of . . . stoney and everything, but they're not very big? I mean, the wall at the end of the garden is bigger than this and Isla's dad built that in like a month.'

Gingerly, almost as if he expected something invisible to stop him, he stepped over the bricks to the other side. 'Um, and also it's not actually a very good stopper?'

'It wasn't always like this. When they built it, it

was huge,' said Eder, grinning at the puppy's earnest face. Poor Joey looked so worried, as if he was really letting them down. 'Tell him, Tor.'

Tor took over. He was walking up and down beside the line of stones in the ground as he talked. 'These bricks are nearly two thousand years old. That's when they started it. By the time they finished it, six years later, the wall was fifteen feet high, like more than two farmer Wolstenholmes, one on top of the other. It ran right across the country for seventy-three miles and split the country in two, north and south, or as they put it, into savages and civilised people.'

Joey tried hard to be impressed, but really? It was just a few bricks. Maybe you had to be a pig to understand it? Perhaps he'd better stay a sheepdog. But that raised other questions. If he wasn't going to be a pig, then what would he do? All his plans had depended on him becoming a pig. He didn't know how to do anything else. That was the trouble with being a sheepdog on a farm with no sheep. What did you do? All the others knew what they were going to do when they grew up, but what could he do? He was a good runner, and a sniffer, but that was it. Being a pig had seemed the obvious answer. But now ... His tummy rumbled and he looked around. He could see a bush growing where the hill dipped down, and it looked like it had some fruit on it.

'Hey, look! A bush! I'm just going to investigate. Who's coming?' he asked hopefully.

Eder and Tor were really happy pottering about among the stones and tracing out where the old fort would once have been. Neither of them paid much attention to the puppy.

'No, we're okay, thanks.' Eder turned back to Tor. 'I wonder why people didn't just knock it down? I mean, if you put a wall up, then humans always want to climb over it. Or knock it down. Same with gates. You could put a gate in the middle of nowhere with nothing on either side and they'd go through it rather than round it. Humans are weird like that.'

Tor nodded. 'Fair, but there were like big gatehouses full of soldiers every mile. And towers in between the gatehouses, and there were sixteen forts scattered along the wall. I think this is where an old fort would have been. You can see a sort of square still in the ground. Anyway, all those places had soldiers in them all the time. It would have been impossible to damage the Wall, or sneak over.'

Joey had scampered down the slope to the bush. It had sort of pointy leaves and lovely purple flowers. But it was the fruit that was interesting the hungry puppy. He'd had nothing but apples and random vegetables for days and days, and he was starving. The trouble was, he just wasn't that keen on apples, and that seemed to be what the pigs ate all the time. This fruit looked a bit more like it. Glistening purple berries, all juicy and ripe-looking – a sort of tempting cross between blueberries and cherries.

He looked up the hill but the two pigs were out of view. He supposed he should call them really, tell them about this lovely sweet snack he'd found, but suddenly he didn't want to. He'd take them some back. He closed his mouth on one of the branches and gently drew his teeth back, scraping the berries into his mouth as he did so. He didn't get very many and they tasted a bit odd, not at all what he'd been expecting.

He was just chewing when he saw something rather curious. Tucked away at the base of the hill, slightly shadowed by the wall, was an opening. A sort of crack or fissure in the hill itself, high enough for a man on a horse to ride through, and just wide enough as well. From what he could see, it led right into the very heart of the earth. What could it be?

Joey felt a powerful urge to investigate. He swallowed the berries and went towards the entrance. It was hard to see, and if he hadn't been looking for it he'd have walked straight past. As he got nearer he could see a sort of glow coming from inside. It wasn't scary though, and the puppy excitedly put his nose inside to see what he could sniff. Nothing much. Better look further. Should he tell the others? No. Wait until he'd investigated, then he'd surprise them. That would teach them not to come with him. Happily he stepped into the hillside.

Tor was just pacing out the outer edge of where the fort would have been when he felt a shiver. He looked up.

'Where's Joey?'

Eder looked around. The puppy was nowhere in sight. 'Joey!' she called out.

The pigs listened intently, but there was no sound other than the wind blowing across the hillside, and the silence of the Wall, stretching away either side of them.

They ran to the top of the hill and looked all around. There was no sign of him.

'He said something about a bush?'

Tor nodded grimly as he looked up and down the Wall. There were bushes everywhere. 'He wouldn't have gone far. He knows better.'

'Joey!' shouted Eder desperately. 'Where can he have got to?'

'He's probably just winding us up. Punishing us for not playing with him,' reassured Tor. 'Come out now! It's not funny, Joey!'

Their voices echoed around the hills, the sound

mocking them as they frantically scanned the landscape for any sign of him.

'Let's split up. I'll go this side, you go the other,' said Tor as he dashed down the hillside. Eder turned and ran the other way.

Tor reached the bush at the bottom of the hill. The fruit looked delicious. He sniffed it for a second but shivered at the familiar smell of deadly nightshade. Then his blood ran cold as he saw, at about Joey's head height, a small branch with all the fruit sucked off.

'Eder!!!!' yelled Tor at the top of his voice.

She was by his side in a second. 'You found him?'

Tor shook his head grimly and pointed at the branch.

Eder sniffed at the bush. 'Deadly nightshade.'

Tor nodded.

'Where is he now?'

They both looked around but there was no sign of Joey anywhere.

'Look.' Eder was looking down at the ground by the bush. There were two berries, which had been squashed, and their poisonous juice was bleeding into the surrounding earth. Eder got down and peered.

Gradually she started slowly heading away from the bush. 'Paw prints. He went this way.'

Tor followed her, both of them studying the faint berry-stained paw prints, which led away from the bush for five or six paces before fading out. 'It looks like he walked right into the hill.'

'I think he must have gone up. Let's go and look at the top. Can you smell him?'

Tor bent down and sniffed at the paw marks. He shook his head grimly and the two of them headed back up to their vantage point on top of the hill. They scanned the whole area but there was nothing moving, just grass gently waving in the breeze, and a little way away, the sparkling reflection of light on water.

Eder leant her head on her brother's shoulder, the two of them trying not to think what might have happened, both their imaginations running wild and picturing the worst.

'Why did he eat those berries?'

'We don't know he did. He's going to come bouncing back any minute, exhausted because he's been chasing some rabbit.'

'Nice try,' said Eder gloomily.

Tor stood up for one last look around, and that's when he saw Joey. Just where they'd been, right by the bush at the bottom of the hill.

'Eder! He's there!'

They both tore down the hill to where the little puppy was lying, shivering, his eyes rolling in his head as his body tried to combat the poison.

'Pigs, pigs, knights!'

'He's mad! Joey, did you eat the berries?'

The puppy didn't seem to even be able to see them. 'Berries, cherries, knights and men, couldn't put Heather together again.'

Eder looked serious. 'Gibberish, he's talking rubbish. We need to wash him out.'

'Eh?'

'Water! We need to wash the poison out.' Eder heaved the puppy onto Tor's back and they raced towards the water they'd seen from the top of the hill.

As they ran the puppy kept babbling nonsense. 'A room, a cave asleep in the mountain, and horses, there were horses all asleep, and each horse had a knight, and each knight had a sword, except for the blizzardy, wizardy one with the beard, longer than Eder's beard, and a stick and a cape and a horn and there was gold all around and all the horses were white and they shone it was so beautiful . . .'

Tor arrived and threw the puppy down into the water. Eder held his head underwater while the puppy struggled and then opened his mouth and swallowed loads of water.

'He needs to be sick,' said Eder frantically, as she hauled him out of the water and he coughed and coughed.

Determinedly, Tor put his trotter down the puppy's throat, wincing as Joey desperately struggled for breath, biting down on the trotter until he could take it no more and was sick all over Tor as he pulled his trotter out. The puppy lay gasping on the floor, but his eyes were back to normal, and apart from his chest heaving, he seemed to be coming round.

'I . . . really . . . hate . . . water . . .' gasped the puppy before falling fast asleep, leaving Eder and Tor laughing with relief as they snuggled either side and did their best to keep Joey warm while he slept.

Joey slept for twelve hours. When he finally woke up he seemed to be fine. A bit wobbly and hungry, but otherwise fine.

'You had us scared, mate,' said Tor in a friendly way. 'Where'd you get to?'

The puppy looked thoughtful, as if he was trying to remember something. 'It's weird,' he said. 'I ate the berries, and yes, I do know how many times you've warned me about that, so no need to go on about it. Anyway, I ate the berries and there was a light coming from a crack in the rock so I went inside the hill.'

Tor looked at Eder who discreetly shook her head. There'd been no crack that they could see. Then again, there was no doubt Joey had emerged from somewhere.

'Inside the hill?' asked Eder.

'Exactly. I followed the light and it was really weird. The light was coming from deep in the mountain.

I've got no idea how it got there because it was way underground, but there was a spooky light.'

'Can I stop you there?' asked Tor crossly. 'Did it never occur to you that we might be a tiny bit worried?'

'You knew where I was. I told you.'

'You didn't say you were going through a secret door into a cave in the mountain.'

The puppy sat up. 'There was a cave. You're right. With knights in armour. All fast asleep, and horses and a wizard. And a king and a queen! There was gold everywhere and a table, and on the table was a big horn and a sword and a ribbon thing.'

'It's a garter,' said Eder gently.

'Sorry?' said Tor looking at her. 'He's talking nonsense.'

'Not nonsense! I saw them! I did!' yelped the outraged puppy.

'It's the story of King Arthur. Rhona told us this story last year. You must have been bunking off,' she said to Tor before turning back to the puppy. 'Do you remember? The legend says that King Arthur and his knights are sleeping in a hidden cave somewhere in

England. When England is in dire peril and has need of them, then they will rise again to do battle against the forces of evil.'

'That's right! That's them! King Arthur and Queen Guineapig!'

'Guinevere,' said Eder gently. 'Someone must cut the garter with the sword and blow the horn. That will break the spell and they will wake up and ride out of the cave to England's rescue. But it's just a story, Joey. It's not true.'

''Tis true! I saw them! The wizard? Rhona never said the wizard bit with the beard.'

'No wonder you remembered it if there were beards,' grinned Tor.

Eder kicked him and turned back to the puppy. 'You were seeing things,' she said gently. 'You'd just eaten some deadly nightshade berries. That's a hallucinogenic plant.'

'What's hallu . . . hallugenic?' asked the puppy.

'It means the poison in it makes you see things. Things that aren't real? You remembered the story and maybe you saw a shape that looked like a door or a sword and your brain made you think you were in the story.'

Joey looked unconvinced.

Eder turned to Tor. 'Go and find some fresh vegetables and plants – we need to get his strength back up. I'll bet there's some wild garlic around here somewhere. It's the end of the season but you might find something.'

Tor pulled her to one side. 'Is that all nonsense then? The knights and such?'

'What do you think?' replied Eder briskly. 'Knights? Buried treasure? Underground caves?'

'But he did disappear. We didn't see him anywhere. Either of us.'

Eder looked at him sternly. 'Nor did we see a secret door leading into the mountainside. Also, even if it were true and he found an underground cave full of King Arthur and knights, England is not in dire need of help. So it's probably a good thing he didn't wake anyone up. I, however, am in dire need of food, so can you please go and find something while I keep an eye on Joey?'

Chapter 10

Otterly Boaring . . .

'Otter!' shouted Joey the next morning. He seemed to be fine again and was running about frantically sniffing things.

Tor and Eder were munching away at a couple of pears. *Taylor's Gold, crunchy, almost buttery flesh with a hint of cinnamon.*

'So, what's the plan, Edds?' Tor said between crunches.

'I mean, we've been looking for ages and we've seen no sign of your father at all. What if he isn't even alive?'

'*Our* father,' said Eder crossly. 'I didn't come all this way for you to get all defeatist and give-uppy just because it's a weeny bit harder than little Tor-y wor-y thought it might be.'

'Do you think your beard will ever grow, by the way? I worry it's getting smaller,' replied Tor.

'I really can smell Otter,' said Joey.

'Does it tickle?' asked Tor seriously. 'Or do you forget it's there? I could number all the hairs if you like? We'd only need to count to ten.'

'Will you stop going on about my beard!' Eder said. 'I know you're jealous and I should be more understanding, but I'm really not in the mood.'

'So I see. I would say keep your hair on, but that would probably be insensitive.'

Eder breathed deeply. 'Keep heading south? Find the mine and see if we can pick up a trace there?'

Tor nodded. 'Makes sense, I suppose.'

'He's here! I'm sniffing him!' said Joey, bouncing up and down.

Eder looked at him wearily. 'Sorry? You can what?'

'I can sniff him! Otter! The one you're looking for.'

'Aitor? You can smell Aitor?' asked Tor in amazement. 'How do you know?'

'It's an old, old smell, but it's definitely pig, and it's more Eder than you. No offence, but she's got a beard, and there's a different smell to her than you. You're a bit, well, less fresh, more sort of grubby? Only this smell isn't that. It's wilder, more hairy. Like Eder, but older. You know?'

Tor and Eder both lifted their snouts and sniffed vigorously.

'You getting anything?' asked Eder.

Tor shook his head. 'Mum used to say your sense of smell was better if you close your eyes. Try that?'

They both did so.

'Can't you smell it?' asked the puppy in frustration. Both piglets opened their eyes. 'Nope, not a thing.'

'Well, it's there. It's grown-up pig smell, Heather mixed up with Eder. Acorns, as well. You know?'

'Where does it go?'

'That way,' said Joey, pointing along the other side of the Wall, his nose quivering.

'Then lead the way.'

They followed the smell for two days. Joey was concentrating really hard as he gambolled along, his nose skimming the ground as he hoovered up the smell. It had been very hard work as the smell had taken them through rivers, and muddy bits, and all sorts of places where Joey had had to work really hard to hang onto the smell, or to find it again once it was lost. Fortunately, now it was getting stronger, and even the less sensitive noses of Tor and Eder could scent it. It was a strong, musty smell, sort of fleshy, and, if they were being honest, not very nice. Was this really what their father smelt like?

Suddenly Joey veered away from the Wall and went sideways, heading into a wood. It was a dark, overgrown forest, one of those places where the floor is always slightly damp, the light never quite breaking through the branches above, and Eder shivered as she followed the snuffling puppy.

'I don't like this,' she muttered to Tor.

'It's fine. It's a wood. Come on, there might even be some acorns.'

Joey was racing through the trees now, ducking under overhanging branches, his paws rustling the leaves as he scampered through them, the two piglets trotting behind. It was getting darker and darker, and Eder was getting more and more nervous.

'Joey!' she shouted.

The puppy stopped and came back to where she was waiting with Tor. 'What's up? The smell's strong. I can sniff it easily.'

'I think we should turn back.'

'What!' Both Tor and Joey were outraged. 'Why?'

Eder looked around and lowered her voice. 'I think someone is watching us.'

Tor looked around them at the trees. 'They wouldn't be able to see anything even if they were. Helloooo! Hi there!' he shouted.

'Shush!' said Eder, but there was no need. Even

shouting, Tor's voice hadn't carried any distance at all. The trees were so thick, the forest so dark and damp, that it just seemed to absorb the sound. It felt like you could shout all day and nobody would ever hear.

The three of them stood there, cloaked in darkness, the silence of the forest lying on them, heavy and oppressive.

'Shall I carry on?' asked Joey. 'The smell's really new and fresh as well. We must be nearly there.'

'We might as well go on, no?' asked Tor, now himself a bit freaked out by the forest. 'I mean, unless you know the way back?'

'Suppose so,' said Eder reluctantly. 'I just wish I didn't feel like we were being watched.'

Joey dashed off and they lost sight of him for a moment, but caught up with him minutes later, not least because he had stopped.

It was pretty much the first time he'd stopped for two days. They were in a small clearing in the middle of the wood. The trees were dense and thick all around, there was no light, and Eder was alarmed to realise she had absolutely no idea where she was, or where the Wall was. They'd taken so many twists and turns she was now completely disoriented. She went forward and stopped by the confused-looking puppy.

'What's up?'

'The smell's gone.'

Eder sniffed. 'I can smell it now.'

'Yes, I know. It's here, in fact there's loads of it, but Otter's not here. Where's Otter? It's like he's vanished.'

Slowly a pile of leaves in the corner started to stir, and out of the middle of it emerged a wild boar. He was covered in golden-brown coarse hair, his snout was well defined and black, and his ears stuck up proudly. He was about Tor's size, and as he looked at them he opened his mouth and snarled, revealing two vicious white tusks protruding from his lower jaw.

'Dad?' said Eder cautiously.

'Hungry,' replied the boar. He ambled slowly towards them, a dribble of saliva hanging from his mouth.

'Hungry,' came a voice from behind them. The pigs turned to see two more boars standing behind them, just inside the clearing.

'Hungry,' came from both sides of the clearing as two more boars came in from the sides.

It was terrifying. Tor and Eder shuffled together, not knowing which way to look, as on all four sides the boars closed in, tusks glinting, and piggy eyes blinking hungrily.

'Joey, get between us!' urged Tor, and the little puppy didn't need to be told twice, scurrying to hide under Tor's reassuring bulk.

Tor cleared his throat. 'We're travellers, looking for our father. His name's Aitor – have you seen him?'

'Hungry!' repeated the boars, now circling round the three terrified animals in the middle. One of them suddenly ran straight at the pigs, aiming for where Joey was sheltering between them.

As he arrived Tor snarled, reared up on his hind legs and lashed out with his trotters. He hit the boar in the face and forced him to retreat, still snarling crossly.

'Where'd you learn to do that?' asked Eder, a bit awestruck.

'Practice,' gulped Tor, trying not to let on how frightened he was. 'I think we should leave. Perhaps if we look like we're leaving they'll let us go?' Keeping Joey between his front trotters, he started to walk back the way they'd come.

The boars blocking the way didn't move.

Tor's legs were quivering as he slowly walked towards them, praying they would move aside and let him through.

'Tor?' said Joey.

'Not now, mate,' gulped the piglet.

'You smell different. You smell like that boy Eder liked.'

The wild boar licked his tusks and bared his teeth at the puppy. 'It's the smell of fear, little one.' He started to walk towards Tor and Joey.

From behind them one of the boars grunted. 'The Seneschal will want these.'

The boar in front licked his lips, and his tusks glinted and gleamed as he came closer. 'If we take them back we'll have to share them, and I'm hungry.'

Taking this as a sign, the other four started to close in as well.

Making sure Joey was between them, Tor backed

into Eder and prepared to rear up again. 'I'll try and distract them, while you take Joey and run. Don't stop for anything,' he whispered as . . .

'RRROOOOAAAAR!'

The trees exploded as something flew out of them and charged barking and roaring into the side of one of the boars. It knocked him flying and then, without a pause, turned and leapt at one of the others, sending him scuttling away before turning back and snarling and leaping at a third. But the boars had had enough of this whirlwind attacker, and all five fled silently off into the wood, leaving the quaking piglets alone with their rescuer.

'Dad!' exclaimed Joey happily as he ran towards Alastair. 'What are you doing here?'

'Hello, son,' said the sheepdog as he nuzzled his son and grinned at the two quaking piglets. 'I need your help.' The puppy looked interested as his dad carried on. 'Shall we get out of this wood? I'm not sure how long those boars will stay away once they see there's only one of me.'

They headed back the way they'd come, Eder and

Tor looking nervously over their shoulders as they went. Alastair had put Joey on his back and was keeping their minds off what had nearly happened by chatting away as he led them out of the wood.

'I had to come and get you because Blackie on the next-door farm needs some help with the sheep – you see, they keep being attacked by the wildcat, and Blackie's getting fed up with it. He's come up with this great idea for flushing him out but he needs our help.' He looked back at his son who was happily sitting on his back and nodding wisely.

There were rustlings in the woods behind Tor and Eder and Tor made a 'speed up' face to the sheepdog.

'Blackie said to me, "We need an excellent sniffer," so I thought I'd better go and tell Joey I need him back here. Took me ages to find you, as I kept losing the scent and then picking it up again, but I'm glad I have. Your mother was a bit worried, you know, when Kirstie said you'd gone off with these two mischief-makers.'

As he said that he grinned back at Tor and Eder, just as they finally emerged from the wood to see the reassuring line of Hadrian's Wall.

'Right, now I slept along here last night and there's some apples and stuff, so let's go and find that as you lot must be starving?'

'How's Mum?' asked Eder.

'Let's get this down you, and then I'll tell you everything,' said Alastair as he uncovered the food he'd left hidden.

Tor hadn't realised how hungry he was and he happily wolfed down the apples. *Johnny Voun, a sweet cider apple, with a subtle anise flavour and a lovely perfume.*

Once they'd eaten their fill they sat around while Alastair told them all what had been going on at the farm. 'Heather's much better. She's up and about and worrying about you both. She was furious with us for letting you go off without a grown-up. We told her you'd be fine, but you know what she's like – worry, worry, worry. George and Ringo are growing up so fast, in fact they all are, and John and Paul fight with each other loads, they really don't seem to get on at all. We hardly see Taylor these days, as she seems to be spending all her time with Angus. You know, Blackie's puppy? He seems nice enough, though.'

He looked down at Joey who'd nodded off and then took the two pigs off to one side.

'Thanks for looking after this one so well. I would have got here sooner but I kept losing you whenever you crossed a stream or a river. We'll set off back home as soon as he wakes up.' He looked at them thoughtfully. 'Are you any closer to finding him?'

'Why?'

'Because I might not have been entirely truthful about Heather. I didn't want to worry Joey, he's only little and he'd probably blame himself because he was the one who fell into the quarry.'

'But she's okay?' asked Tor and Eder together.

'She had a bit of a relapse. She's fine, but she's just . . . not quite herself. She's missing you. So, if you don't find him soon, then maybe come back, yeah?'

Tor looked at Eder. Once again, he was so glad she was with him.

An hour later Alastair and Joey set off. Joey hadn't been that upset that his friends weren't coming – he was just thrilled to be going home, and excited about the prospect of hunting down the wildcat. They listened to his voice fading out as he talked nonstop to his dad.

'And I still can't swim, but we met this dolphin, he was really friendly and he thinks I should learn to swim because it's really useful and I've changed my mind about what I'm going to be when I grow up. I mean, it'd be fun to be a pig, but I think I really want to be a sheepdog. Because I'm good at running, and I'm a really good sniffer, I mean, I followed those boars all the way into the middle of the wood. How do you tell the difference between a Bearded pig and a boar? They seem to smell really similar . . .'

'You thinking what I'm thinking?' asked Eder as they watched the pair of them heading up the hill.

'Usually,' answered Tor. 'What are you thinking?'

Eder paused for a moment. 'Be weird to have a dad.'

'Nice weird?'

Eder shrugged. 'Dunno. It didn't do us any harm Otter not being there.'

Tor nodded. 'D'you think Mum's okay?'

They stood in thoughtful silence for a while.

'By the way,' said Tor. 'You know Joey said I smelt like your friend, and the boar said it was the smell of fear?'

Eder nodded.

'He was right as it happens. I was terrified. So what was your friend scared of?'

'Finn?' Eder looked thoughtful. 'Being left, I guess? Maybe he always suspected his dad wouldn't come back?' She thought for a minute. 'At least we didn't ever know Aitor, so we never knew what we were missing.'

Tor nodded. 'Mum did though.'

They watched as in the distance Alastair picked up Joey by the scruff of his neck and put him on his back. Then the dogs were on top of the hill, and suddenly they were lost from view as they headed down the other side.

'No regrets?' asked Tor.

Eder looked at the yew tree that was sheltering them. 'Not about the farm.'

Tor looked a bit surprised. 'You still missing Finn?'

Eder rested her snout on her trotters and nodded sadly.

'He really got into your beard, didn't he?'

'The expression is "got under your skin", not "into your beard",' said Eder wearily.

'Not any more,' replied Tor gleefully.

Eder turned away. She was hunched over and as Tor looked across she started shaking.

'Are you okay, Tufty?'

Eder ignored him and carried on quietly sobbing.

'Eder? What's wrong?'

'Go away!'

'Hey, what's up?' asked Tor, suddenly feeling really guilty.

'You know what's wrong!' sniffed Eder.

'It was a joke, just a joke, Edds.'

'It's not a joke!' Eder turned on him, tears in her eyes. 'You know how self-conscious I've always been about my beard, you *know* it! You know I've always worried about it, and you won't ever leave me alone about it! You know I hate my beard . . . At least, I used to . . .' She looked at her devastated guilty brother, grinned at him and winked before delivering the knock out. 'But now it's really growing on me!'

Chapter 11

The Seneschal . . .

The two piglets searched and searched with no luck at all. The trail seemed to be completely dead. By now it was the beginning of December, the run-up to Christmas, and decorations were going up on the local houses, bauble-clad trees appearing in windows, and even the nights didn't seem so dark because of all the lights.

'Humans are weird,' said Tor as he and his sister watched two hatted, scarved, gloved and coated children staggering out of their front door carrying a huge reindeer made of see-through plastic. As Eder looked thoughtful, the children passed the reindeer to their dad who clambered up a ladder and arranged it on the roof of the house.

'Okay!' he called out, and inside someone flicked a switch and the reindeer lit up, flashing and twinkling as the children cheered and clapped.

'Santa won't miss that!' said their dad as he climbed down from the ladder.

Eder looked at the twinkling reindeer, the lights blinking and flashing as it sparkled magically. Why was she here? What was she doing wandering around England when there was somewhere she was needed? Somewhere she absolutely should be. Somewhere where stars shone through the leaves of a tree and a boy told her stories about bears, Christmas trees and queens. She got to her trotters.

'Let's go.'

'Where?' asked Tor.

'To find him. Then we can go home.'

'Otter?' asked Tor. 'You got a plan?'

'I do.' She set off away from the house.

Tor trotted after her. 'You going to share the plan? Tell me where we're headed?'

'We're going back to the wood.'

Tor scampered around in front of her and blocked the way forward. 'Woah, woah, woah! The wood? You mean the terrifyingly scary wood with the damp and the darkness and, oh yes, the wild boars who wanted to eat us!!! *That* wood?'

'That's the one.'

'Umm, how shall I put this?' He paused. 'Why?!!'

'Because they know where the Seneschal is. And he, despite maybe being a wolf, and definitely being truly terrifying, may know where Dad is.'

'Can I just say again, one more time, slowly, so you understand, they tried to eat us!!!!'

'Do you have a better idea?'

'Yes, actually.'

'Go on,' said Eder.

'Anything else!'

'Then I'll go on my own.'

'That's not fair.'

'Why not? You don't have to come.'

'Because you'll get eaten and I'll feel guilty for ever that I didn't get eaten with you.'

'So, chum me?'

Tor sighed. He supposed she did have a point. 'Can we at least have a plan?'

'A plan? My brother is suggesting a plan?'

'Ha ha. Listen, what about if you go and talk to them, not least because you look like a wild boar anyway.'

'Do not!' squealed the offended Eder.

'Yes, well, I know your magnificent beard will one day single you out as not a boar, but at the moment, even you have to admit, it doesn't really jump out at you.'

'It takes time to grow,' said Eder defensively. 'But okay, fine, I'll admit I do look a tiny bit more like a wild boar than you do. Despite my beard.'

'Fine. So how about you go and talk to them. I'll be watching from a hiding place, and if there's any trouble I'll tear in and rescue you. You know, like Alastair did?'

Eder didn't look convinced. 'That's a terrible idea. We need to be taken prisoner. At least, I do.'

'How does that work?'

'I get caught. They take me to the Seneschal, I find out where Dad is, we find Dad and go home. End of.'

'So what do I do?'

'You wait. If I don't come back you go home.'

'What if they eat you?'

'They won't.'

'Because?'

'I'll talk to them.'

Tor wasn't convinced. 'That's a rubbish plan.'

'You got a better one?'

'I still think sticking together is better.'

'That's because you're a boy. Less emotionally mature, therefore less able to function on your own.'

'I just think someone should warn the wild boars how smug you are before they eat you. You might give them a stomach ache.'

'Well, well, well,' came a voice from behind them. 'What have we here?'

It was a hunting party of boars who had snuck up while Tor and Eder were busy arguing.

Eder turned to the boar. His tusks glinted. 'We have urgent information for the Seneschal. I insist you take us to him.'

'What is it?' asked the boar.

'It's for his ears only,' answered Eder determinedly.

'You think I'm stupid?'

'No, but I think you know when to be sensible,' replied the piglet.

'Perhaps I do, but I don't need two of you. And I do need some food. So which of the two of you has the information?'

'Eder, do you remember those Roman war pigs?' asked Tor. 'The ones with the elephants?'

Eder looked blank for a second and then she nodded. Without any warning she suddenly started to squeal. It was a horrible noise, the high-pitched squeal of a pig in real pain, and even though the boars weren't elephants, they were terrified.

Three of them ran away and even the leader hid his head between his trotters and howled at her to stop. He begged her, he pleaded, he implored, and finally he just sobbed, 'Please . . .'

So Eder stopped squealing and the other boars slowly came back, looking at her in alarm, terrified that she might start again at any moment.

But Eder had no intention of starting again. The squealing had done its job. Tor was gone.

The boars huffed and puffed and looked around for him but to no avail, and now that he was missing they couldn't take the chance that the Seneschal might find out they had eaten a prisoner with information for him. They surrounded Eder and started marching her south.

From the bushes, Tor watched and waited.

He followed them all afternoon and evening and well into the night. They seemed to be heading slightly south of the Wall but staying within about half a mile of it, and it wasn't hard to stay hidden but keep them in view.

They finally stopped at the foot of a hill, outside

what looked to Tor like the entrance to a cave. Although the moon was full it was pretty black and he crept closer to hear what they were saying.

The leader lay down on the ground. 'Three of you stay by her. We'll sleep here tonight.'

'Why are we stopping?' asked Eder wearily. She was exhausted, hungry and quite scared.

'The Seneschal will be sleeping,' said the boar, jerking his snout towards the cave. 'Not worth our while to disturb him.' He looked up as the hoot of an owl pierced the night air.

'That's a strange owl,' muttered the chief boar.

Tor! Eder grinned to herself. It was all she needed. She wasn't alone.

'So he's in there, is he? The Seneschal?' asked Eder, talking unnaturally loudly.

The boar grunted.

'On his own?'

'There's others, but nobody sleeps near him.'

'So is this the only way in?'

'Yes. Why do you want to know?' said the boar.

'No reason,' replied Eder innocently.

165

The boars were snoring, but Eder was awake as she saw a shadowy figure tip-trotter towards her. She tried to move, but the guard boars stirred and sat up grumbling, so she quickly lay down and pretended to be asleep.

Tor slipped into the cave and was instantly at home. It was like the quarry at home, but with a roof. There was algae on the wall which must have trapped the daylight because it was glowing gently, and he was fairly sure if he oinked loudly it would echo excellently.

In front of him was a big chamber – and his first problem. There were at least twenty corridors leading off the chamber. Which one should he take?

He walked around the chamber, listening at each of the entrances for any sound. There was nothing. He walked around the chamber again. Something smelt really nice. What was it? He stopped and sniffed properly. Woah! A chestnut! On the ground! In front of him! Waiting to be— His mouth was suddenly full of saliva. How long had it been since he'd had a chestnut? All the trees around the Wall

had been picked bare, with not a nut for miles –
Eder reckoned it was the boars who'd eaten them
all. So what was one doing inside the cave? And
why hadn't it been eaten already? Almost as if she
were there with him, he heard his mother's voice
telling him the old rhyme.

If you see an apple on a chair,
It's likely someone put it there.

The chestnut wasn't there by accident. It was too
out of place. Like an apple on a chair. It must have
been put there by someone.

And then not eaten.

By greedy boars trooping in and out of here all
day?

It must be marking something. Tor looked at the
doorway 'marked' by the chestnut. It seemed very like
all the others. Just then, a shaft of light struck the
back wall above his head. It was morning. Soon the
boars would be getting up. He could wait and see
which tunnel they took, or he could follow his instincts.

Cautiously he stepped into the tunnel. Suddenly
he stopped, retraced his steps and carefully moved

the chestnut so it was outside a different tunnel. Then he set off again.

Within minutes it was totally dark. The light from the algae on the walls was left behind, and Tor was moving through thick darkness. He loved it. He was back in the caves and underground pools around his quarry at home, exploring, relying on his senses, his snout and his trotters. He closed his eyes to make his snout more sensitive, and picked up speed. He could feel the walls of the tunnel either side of him, as it was fairly narrow, and he hoped he'd been right about the chestnut. He didn't fancy being trapped with an angry boar in this corridor.

Something was in there with him.

Okay, this wasn't funny any more. He turned and tried to head back the way he'd come, but he was confused. He ran into a wall, and then another. Where was the opening? He raced again but couldn't find it. He skidded on the straw and bumped into the wall again. The panic was building.

'Edddder!' Tor wailed.

'Stop!' came a low growl from the dark.

Tor froze. 'Who's there?' he stuttered.

'I am the Seneschal. Who are you and how dare you disturb me?'

'I'm really sorry. I'm looking for my sister Eder – that is, I mean, she's outside, but I'm in here to—'

'Who are you?'

'I'm T-t-tor.'

'Don't stutter. Say that again. Your name.'

'Tor. Tor Duroc, like my mother.'

'Who is your mother?'

'Heather, Heather Duroc. She's called that because she's a Duroc pig and when she was little she—'

'She used to eat heather,' interrupted the darkness. 'I've heard the story. I don't believe you are her son. From what I've heard, no son of hers would abandon his sister and go off on his own.'

'I am her mother! I mean she's my son. Mother.'

'What is her favourite food?'

'Apples!'

'What is her favourite apple?'

'Um, er . . . er, Braeburn.'

'Liar!'

'No, no stop, it's a S-s-spartan! Deep-red skin with a pineapple taste and crisp, white flesh!'

'Who is her best two-legged friend?'

'Isla. Isla Wolstenholme. Farmer Wolstenholme's daughter. Only he's not a farmer now. He used to be, but after Mr Busby went bankrupt and we got the farm back he became a jelly-maker. Only you can't say "Jelly-maker Wolstenholme" because it sounds a bit weird,' babbled Tor in complete terror.

There was a pause, and Tor could almost feel the darkness thinking. When it spoke again there was a grim satisfaction in the voice.

'So she did it.'

'Who? Did what?'

'Your mother. She got the farm back.'

'Er, kind of. The chicken farmer was doing something dodgy and everyone found out so he got arrested. Mum just found a sword or something.'

'What happened. Tell me.'

'There was like this big thing with Isla's old school and loads of children were there apparently. They'd all like come to see the farm or something. It was on my birthday. Like my real one. The one when I was born. Not like when I was one, or two, I mean my actual—'

'Your birth-day, I understand. Get on with it.'

'Apparently Mum was like cross because the chickens were being mistreated and not being like fed or looked after properly.'

'Will you stop saying "like" every third word please. It's incorrect, unnecessary and quite irritating.'

'Sorry, yeah, right. Anyway she like freed, sorry, she freed them, the chickens that is, and when they got out, all the people realised Mr Busby'd been lying to them and like arrested him.'

'So Isla's father bought the farm back?'

'Yeah. The sword Mum found was, like – sorry! – was really old so they sold it.'

The darkness breathed heavily. When it spoke again the voice was a bit wavery. 'So why are you here?'

'She's not well. She—'

'What's wrong with Eder?'

'Nothing, Eder's fine.'

'You said she was ill.'

'No, it's my mum who's ill. Heather. Eder's my sister.'

There was silence from the darkness. 'You have a sister called Eder?'

'Yes.'

'And your name is Tor?'

'Yeah. Well, it's short for Aitor, which apparently was my dad's name, but I didn't want to be called after him so everyone calls me Tor.'

'Why not?'

'What?'

'Why not be called after him?'

'My dad?'

'Yes.'

'Because he's a coward. My mum really loved him and he abandoned her. He left her to bring up two piglets all on her own. Why would I want to be like him?'

There was a long silence again. When the darkness spoke again it was tinged with regret and pain.

'Maybe he couldn't be with her?'

'Why not? I'm not being funny, but he just had to turn up.'

'How old are you?'

'I'm two. Just. Eder's two also, but she's older than me. By like a minute. Hang on, why are you asking me all these questions? Did you know my dad? Have you seen him?'

The voice was silent. Tor peered into the blackness but he couldn't see anything.

At that very moment, they heard the sound of pounding trotters echoing up the corridor and a panting boar galloped into the chamber.

'Your majesty?'

'Yes?'

'Is everything okay?'

'It was fine. Until you came blundering in here. I presume you've found it?'

'Um, no, but—'

'Then there'd better be an extremely good reason for this.'

'Someone moved the chestnut, sir. We thought you might be in danger.'

'Me? In danger? Only from idiocy. Get out.'

'Yes, sir. Right, sir. So nobody's come this way, sir?'

'Get out!' roared the darkness and the boar fled back down the corridor.

'That was me actually. Um ... I moved the chestnut. Sorry.'

'Why?'

'Because I thought it was probably important. You see, my mother told me this thing years ago – I think it was an expression of my father's – about an apple and a chair. She couldn't understand it, but it's basically saying that things are there for a reason and so I thought the chestnut probably was marking which tunnel—'

'If you see an apple on a chair,
It's likely someone put it there.'

As it interrupted him, the figure rose out of the darkness and came towards the terrified Tor. It had four feet, and from what Tor could make out, the creature was huge. The hair looked stiff, and far from looking like a wolf, it looked more like . . . a pig?

Surely . . . it couldn't be . . . ?

'Hello, son.'

Chapter 12

Talk to the Cave . . .

'Dad?'

Tor was momentarily speechless, and then the questions started to come thick and fast.

'What's going on? Is it really you? How come you're here? Where have you been? Why didn't you come and find us? Mum was really upset. She thought you were dead. Who are these boars? How could you just stay here?'

'I will answer all your questions, but first we must find your sister.'

'They've got her. They were bringing her to you.'

Aitor walked to the door and bellowed for one of the wild boars. Seconds later, one trotted into the chamber.

'Yes, Seneschal?'

'Where is the prisoner? The girl pig.'

The boar looked astonished. 'How did you know about her?'

'I know many things, little boar. Now bring her to me.'

Minutes later Eder was led into the room. Aitor dismissed the boar and then addressed himself to Eder.

'Your brother is here. He is safe and well.'

'Tor?'

'Hi, Edds. Um, this is Dad.'

Eder gasped. 'Dad? But you're the Seneschal!'

177

'Yes. But I'm also your father.'

'How is that even possible?'

'You sound so like your mother. Do you look like her?'

'Er, well, I'm sort of more . . . bearded.'

Aitor gasped. 'I have a bearded daughter . . . I never . . .' He cleared his throat and seemed quite choked with emotion. 'May I . . . touch . . . ?'

Eder nodded.

Aitor didn't move.

'He's blind, remember . . .' whispered Tor, and Eder jumped.

She walked towards her father and pressed her snout against the side of his face. Very gently he stroked her beard with his.

'You have the Ezkurra beard,' he said, his voice catching.

'But it's so tufty,' muttered Eder.

'From tufty sprouts do great beards grow,' said her father wisely.

'I thought that was oak trees from acorns?'

'Why do you think your name is Ezkurra? It

178

literally means "the place of acorns".' He turned back to Tor. 'You said your mother was ill. What's happened? Is she all right?'

'She dived into a river to save a puppy but swallowed a lot of mud and stuff and they think something in the water made her ill.'

'Dogs! They are such irresponsible creatures.'

'Actually, it was me,' said Tor.

'Did you push the dog?'

'No, but he does what I tell him. I was stupid. Mum being ill is my fault.'

'Taking responsibility for your actions is good. I'm glad to see you're living up to your name.'

'Aitor?' said Tor bitterly. 'Mum said it meant "good father". That's, that's . . . what is it, Edds?'

'It's ironic,' muttered Eder in agreement.

'Actually I meant Tor – the name you have chosen for yourself. People say that because names are given at birth they are random and not important, and yet we all make sense of the names we are given. Or we change them. A tor for instance is a mighty hill or rocky peak. It is solid, dependable, reliable. Yet Sir

Tor was also one of the noblest of King Arthur's knights. He was the illegitimate son of Sir Pellinore. That means his father wasn't with his mother when he was born. Tor made his own way in the world, even to the point of being knighted, and all without any of the benefit of his father's name or guidance. You knew nothing of that, and yet you suit the name perfectly.'

'You said you'd answer our questions. Mum was so unhappy. She misses you so much. Why didn't you come and find us?'

Aitor was silent for a long time. When he eventually spoke it seemed to come from a long way away.

'I couldn't.'

'Why not?'

'Just believe me. I wanted to, but I couldn't.'

'Don't give me that. You escaped from London Zoo and travelled north all the way to Gateshead. Mum made it back, so why couldn't you?'

'When we left London I had your mother to help me. By your mother's side, anything is possible. Whereas when I was alone . . .'

'So you gave up? You just stayed here? With these boars? How come you're their leader anyway? Are they scared of you?'

'They aren't very bright. Also, they wanted a leader. Animals often do. Like humans. Someone tells them what to do and they do it.'

'What are they doing then? You asked that boar earlier if he'd found "it". What's "it"?'

Aitor took a deep breath. 'There is a cave near here, somewhere beneath the wall, and in that cave sleep a king, a wizard and eighty knights. He is the King under the mountain. He has many names, but you probably know him as Arthur. He and his knights are sleeping until they are called upon to save England in its time of direst need.'

Tor was about to say something, but Eder gave him a look and he kept quiet, as Aitor continued, 'I thought if I found the cave I could get Arthur's magician to return my sight. Stupid, I know, but somehow I couldn't live a real life with your mother until I could see.'

'Mum doesn't care if you're blind or not.'

'But I do. For years in the zoo I lived half a life

181

and then she came along and changed everything. She is the most amazing pig I've ever met. I wanted to be worthy of her.'

'By not being with her? That makes sense,' said Tor sarcastically.

'Were you scared?' asked Eder. It was the first thing she'd said for a long time.

Aitor hung his head. 'Scared, old and tired. It seemed easier to hide here in the dark than to try and find your mother when I can't even see where I'm going.'

'But we can see,' said Tor. 'And Mum doesn't care whether you can see or not. She loves you. You should hear her talk about you, every night a different bedtime story about Aitor. Our father who gave his life so that we could be born free.'

Eder was sure in the darkness she saw a flash of white as the boar smiled. 'My Scheherazade.'

'So let's go.' Eder got up. 'Come on, it's quite a walk home, so let's get started.'

Aitor shrunk back into the room. 'I can't come.'

'What! Why not?'

'I'm too old.'

'So we probably shouldn't waste any more time?'

'I've been in this cave for nearly two years. I doubt I can even walk any more.' In the darkness Eder saw the mighty boar's head drop.

'Please come.' She said it very quietly. 'We've come all this way to find you. To find our dad.'

'It was your choice to come.'

'Yes, it was,' said Eder, 'but we could only make that choice because of you.'

Tor took over. 'You made sure that we were born free. You gave us that choice, so now we're making it.'

'This is blackmail,' said Aitor.

'I prefer to think of it as love,' replied Eder. 'You've got these boars all searching for a king who's sleeping in a cave. Well, we've found *our* king, and we want to take him home. Mum's not well, and she really really wants to see you, so would you please just come home?'

Aitor shook his head. 'Fine! You are just like her! So good at arguing.' He stood up and started shaking his legs to get the blood flowing again. 'First problem, even if I can walk, how will we get past the boars?'

'What do you mean?' asked Eder.

'I can't just walk out. I am their leader. I've been promising them all sorts. I've told them the cave's a place of magic, filled with gold and precious stones.'

'What do boars want with gold and precious stones?' asked Tor.

Aitor roared with laughter. 'What indeed? All I can think is that they are either not very clever or, like magpies, they like shiny things. Anyway, they won't let me leave. If I suggest there is no cave of jewels and that I'm off home, they would feel stupid and lash out at the one who made them feel that way.'

'I'll talk to them,' said Tor. 'Make them see sense.'

'I've got a better idea,' said Eder thoughtfully. She turned to Aitor. 'If I can get you past the boars, will you at least try? What have you got to lose?'

Aitor turned away, muttering about emotional blackmail and annoying piglets.

Eder asked her dad to tell all the boars to assemble in the cave the following morning and she would address them. She and Tor had worked out a plan, and by the time she and her father emerged into the algae-lit cave, there were nearly a hundred wild boars gathered around, all looking tusked and grumpy, and all staring with hatred at Eder. There were low murmurings of discontent and a few tusks were waved at her.

Eder stepped forward and tried to speak, but the mutterings just got louder. Aitor stepped forward and sat on his haunches. Instantly everyone was silent.

'Noble boars!' began Eder. 'The Seneschal has called me to help. The cave we seek is close at hand. Your quest is nearly at an end. There is more gold there than anyone can carry, but the resting place of the once and future king is hard to find, and even harder to enter. It is protected by powerful magic.'

'We've looked everywhere!' cried one boar.

Other voices joined in.

'It's too well hidden.'

'We can't find it.'

'How do we know it's even there? How can you find it when we can't?'

Eder ignored them. 'There is a fort a few miles from here along the Wall. It is marked on the ground and rises high with a hill leading down below. Its name is Sewingshields.'

'I know that place!' shouted one boar. 'There's nothing there. I've looked all round there. It's just stones and grass.'

'Quiet!' roared Aitor. 'Let her speak.'

'If you go down the hill by the fort, you will come to a fold in the ground. The hill rises up behind you, and hidden in the fold of the hillside is a crack in the rock that leads deep into the mountainside. The treasure lies within. But this is old, old magic, protected by druids and wizards from long ago. They have enchanted the very earth to protect what lies within. To get inside the mountain, to find the cave, you must eat a single berry from the bush which grows by the entrance to the cave itself.'

Eder couldn't believe they were falling for this nonsense, but it seemed to be working. One of the boars turned to the one who'd spoken out. 'Is there a bush? With berries?' The other boar nodded enthusiastically.

'Once you have eaten a berry, the crack in the rock becomes visible and you can enter within. But only those who eat a berry will be able to enter the cave and find the treasure.'

'Why should we believe you?' shouted a voice.

'Ask the land if I speak the truth.'

'How?'

'Ask the cave a question. Go on.'

One of the boars cleared his throat. 'Er . . . cave. Is she right?'

This was the bit of the plan Eder was most worried about. She knew the boars would want some proof and Tor had assured her he could find the perfect spot. She prayed he had.

No sound came. The boar laughed. 'Hey, cave!' he shouted a bit louder, 'Is she telling the truth?' There was no answer. Eder was getting slightly nervous, but outwardly she tried to stay as calm as possible.

The boar turned round and said to the others,

'Maybe I don't speak cave? Does anyone speak cave?' There was laughter among the boars but then there was a low rumble. 'What was that?'

The rumble came again, louder this time, deeper, louder. The boars looked around. Then suddenly there was a roar which rolled deafeningly around the inside of the cave, echoing and reverberating as it bounced off the stone and made everyone cower as the very walls of the cave seemed to shake with sound.

Then as the echoes died away and the boars hunched in terror and awe, a low, rumbled 'She speaks the truth,' floated through the cave, the sound seeming to come out of the very stones and hanging in the air like smoke.

'To the cave!' shouted Eder in triumph, and as one all the boars turned and raced out of the cave, gabbling as they went, leaving Eder and Aitor surrounded by the dying echoes.

Chapter 13

Chestnuts and Cuckoos

'Phew,' said Eder as Tor clambered down from a perch he'd found, high up on the walls of the cave. 'Nice work, Tor.' She grinned at him. 'How did you make that roar?'

Tor grinned back. 'It's the same as the quarry at home. You've just got to find the right spot and then roar from the chest.'

Aitor was sitting quietly. 'What happens when they can't find the cave?' he asked.

'We'll be long gone,' said Eder. 'The magic bush I told them about is Belladonna, deadly nightshade. They'll be fine, one berry won't be dangerous to them but I'm reckoning they'll have some quite bad tummy aches for at least a day before they realise we've gone.'

Tor nodded. 'Once we cross the river Tay I reckon we're safe.'

'Don't count on it,' said Aitor gloomily. 'It takes a lot to put a boar off the hunt.'

It was a good thing they had a head start, as Aitor was in no condition to walk fast, and although he marched doggedly, their progress was painfully slow and Eder kept looking behind them nervously.

The first day they didn't get far, but Hadrian's Wall was behind them, so Tor said you could argue they were in Scotland, or at least 'back home with the savages'. That night they stopped under a spreading chestnut tree with wide branches and a few hardy chestnuts still surviving.

'The oldest tree in Europe is a chestnut tree,' said

Aitor as they sat around that evening. 'It's called the Hundred Horse Chestnut, after a princess who sheltered under it with her knights and their horses when they got caught in a storm. It's in Italy, on the slopes of Mount Etna. The Sicilian Black Swine who live there are one of the most intelligent of all species of pig. They're similar-looking to wild boars, but in character they couldn't be more different.'

Tor was looking at Eder. 'Eder thinks you're wrong.'

Aitor turned to his daughter. 'Don't let your brother speak for you. What is it?'

'Um, some people say the oldest tree in Europe is actually the Fortingall yew tree. Estimates put it at between two and five thousand years old. It's in Perthshire. I'm sure your tree is really old as well.'

'How interesting,' said Aitor thoughtfully. 'You really are so very like your mother. So wise, and yet you let me ramble on when you know much better. Why is that?'

Eder thought for a moment. 'Mum used to say it was disrespectful to contradict other animals.'

'Even when they're wrong? How typical of your

mother. Sensitive, considerate and selfless. It's no wonder you two are such exceptional piglets. So, Eder, tell me more about this yew tree.'

So Eder talked and talked, and gradually the conversation turned to Finn, and Eder's eyes lit up as she told them all about him, and how even though she'd only known him a short time she really, really liked him. 'He calls me Iona, because obviously I can't tell him my name is Eder so he asked the yew tree what I should be called and he pretended the yew tree said Iona, so that's what he calls me,' said Eder, blushing as she told the story.

'That's an excellent name for you,' said Aitor happily. 'Do you like it?'

Eder nodded, still a bit embarrassed. 'He said it was an island, where there were loads of yew trees or something?'

'He's right. It's an island formed of the oldest rock in the world. It's also the most spiritual place in Scotland, where Saint Columba settled and preached Christianity. I have always wanted to visit it. Interestingly he exiled cows from the Island. Pigs were fine, but no cows were allowed. He claimed it was because they caused mischief, but I think he just couldn't bear to be around such gormless animals.'

'What's gormless mean?' asked Tor.

'It means just not very bright. A bit slow.'

'Gullible. You know, like Kirstie and the moths?' added Eder.

Tor grinned as he remembered.

'How did you know about the cave?' asked Aitor.

'Joey found it. You know, the puppy? Well, I mean he said he had. But he was talking gibberish because he'd eaten the belladonna berries so we didn't believe him. Why? Do you think it might really be there?'

Aitor smiled sadly. 'Sometimes the things we look for all our lives are under our noses all the time. The Tin Man's heart in *The Wizard of Oz*, indeed, the Lion's courage as well. They already had those things, but they just needed to realise they did. Just like you two made me see that I don't need my sight to be with Heather. I just need to get there. It sounds so obvious now. How can it have taken me so long to see it?'

'Maybe seeing things is a problem for you?' said Tor.

Eder gave him an angry look, but Aitor roared with laughter. 'You are so like your mother as well! She laughs at me all the time, and never ever lets me be pompous.' He paused for a minute. 'Iona and Tor – they are names to be proud of, so make sure you wear them well.'

'Dad?' said Eder. 'What's stronger than God, more evil than the Devil, the rich want it, the poor have it, and if you eat it you die?'

Aitor thought for a moment. 'Nothing. Why do you ask?'

Eder grinned at him. 'No reason. Thanks, Dad!'

The next morning Tor was woken up by Aitor nuzzling him.

'Get up! Come on, both of you.'

'What's up? Is it the boars?'

Aitor was shaking his head. 'There's an electrical storm coming. Big one.'

Tor looked at the sky. It was a bit dark, but then it was December in Scotland, a season when usually it felt as though the sun came out, took one look around and went back to bed. 'Doesn't look like it.'

Aitor tutted. 'Can't you smell it? Use your snout.'

'You can smell a storm?'

Aitor nodded. 'So can you. Close your eyes and sniff deeply.'

Tor did so.

'Can you smell that sharp, fresh scent?'

'Yes, what is it?'

'Ozone. Lightning splits the air and creates ozone. The storm pushes the smell ahead of it. I'd say it'll be here in about half an hour. We should get out from under this tree.'

Exactly twelve minutes later, and with no warning, the storm hit them hard. Aitor and Eder were crossing a field and Tor was lagging behind. Aitor felt the first drops and heard the thunder as the lightning tore open the sky right above their heads.

'Eder. Where can we shelter?'

'Follow my voice – there's a tree just here,' said

Eder, running towards the tree as fast as she could go.

'No, Eder! Stop!' roared Aitor as Eder dashed under the tree. 'Get away from the tree!' As Eder tried to hear what he was saying, forked lightning shot out of the sky and struck the tree, which exploded outwards, the trunk shattering and bits of bark flying in all directions.

'We need to get low. Is there a ditch? Where's Tor?' said Aitor as Eder arrived, her legs shaking from her narrow escape.

'There's a river bed over here.'

'Perfect. Where's your brother?' repeated Aitor as they galloped and then slid into the river bed.

'He's coming, but the lightning's just behind him!' cried Eder as she peered over the edge of the river bed.

'Tor!' bellowed Aitor. 'When the lightning strikes, stand on two trotters!'

Tor was racing across the field, but he was being pursued by the lightning – it seemed to be just behind him, shooting down in forks as he hared towards them. He was nearly there, and they could see his terrified eyes as the sky above crackled with electricity.

'Trotters, Tor!' shouted Eder.

But just as Tor reared up onto his hind legs, a fork of lightning struck the ground about three metres to his left and he jerked as if he'd been hit and was flung into the air.

'No!' howled Eder, and before Aitor could stop her she'd leapt out of the ditch and run over to her brother, who was lying motionless on the ground. 'Tor, Tor!' she wailed, snuffling at him and nudging him desperately. 'Wake up! Please!'

Aitor arrived at her side, just as Tor groaned and rolled over.

'What happened?' he moaned. 'Did I get hit?'

'Ground current,' said Aitor. 'When lightning strikes, it can spread underground and come up anywhere it finds a point of contact. Four-legged animals get hit in four places. Rearing up like that probably saved your life.' He leant down and helped Tor get back to his shaky trotters. 'I think two lucky escapes will do for one day. Come on, the storm's passing, so let's see if we can find something to eat.'

After that they made good progress, and it wasn't long before they reached Loch Tay. Aitor was pressing on uncomplainingly, but the walking was obviously very hard for him, and occasionally Tor saw him wincing with tiredness at the end of the day. They skirted around Loch Tay and had just climbed a hill the other side when they heard the distant, familiar call of a cuckoo. Tor was jumping about imitating it, and even Eder was grinning at his antics, but Aitor was looking very serious.

'Dad? What's wrong?' asked Eder.

'That noise,' he replied.

'It's only a cuckoo. What's up?'

'It's December. When did you ever hear a cuckoo in December?'

'Oh, yeah. They've all migrated. So what is it?'

'It's a wild boar's hunting call. Means they've picked up our trail.'

And sure enough, when they looked behind them,

in the distance they could see wild boars spread out across the landscape, all galloping towards them. There must have been twenty or thirty of them, and they were closing fast.

Chapter 14

The Breaking of the Chumship

'Dad, come on! There's like thirty boars! Come on!'

'Don't use "like" like that. I don't like it,' replied Aitor calmly.

'Okay, I won't, but can we *go*?'

'You go. Run now, and I will stay and distract them.'

'Don't be ridiculous!'

'It's me they want.'

'We want you more! Come on!'

'I'm old, children, old and tired. Perhaps it is my time.'

'I see what Mum meant about you being pompous!' Tor got behind Aitor and started pushing, but the massive pig was too big to move.

'Fine,' said Eder. 'If you stay then we all stay. Oh look, the boars have reached the side of the loch. Won't be long now. Still, if Dad says we're all going to go together then that's what we'll do, eh, Tor?'

'Yup. Shame really, I was looking forward to seeing the farm again. Oh well.'

'Fine!' shouted the exasperated Aitor. 'Where are we going?'

'Follow me!' shouted Eder and ran off, oinking just loudly enough so that Aitor could hear her over the baying of the hunting boars.

Eder felt so happy – she had been dreaming of this moment for weeks. She knew the route so well, and somehow she just knew where Finn would be. She tore through the wood, ducked and dived through the gravestones, trusting Tor to guide Aitor, and arrived, oinking furiously, at the yew tree.

She barely had time to stop before a figure was leaping out of the tree and racing towards her, his arms wide open. 'Iona! You're back! Hooray!'

She leapt into his arms and snuffled him frantically, tickling him with her beard as he patted and stroked her coarse hair.

'Your beard's grown, and your stripes are gone! Where have you been – it's been weeks! What's going on? I've got so much to tell you. What?' He stopped and looked into her eyes. 'What's up? You look terrified.'

Eder nodded behind her to where Tor and Aitor were panting. 'Hello again. You've lost the puppy. But . . . ?' He looked at Aitor, then at Eder. 'This must be your father. Is it?'

Eder scrunched happily and Finn walked over and held out his hand to Aitor. Aitor didn't react and Finn gently touched his sightless eyes in wonder. 'You're blind, aren't you? You have an extraordinary daughter, sir. I am honoured to call her my friend.'

The call of a cuckoo made all three pigs prick up their ears.

'A cuckoo? In December?' said Finn, and looked at Eder curiously. She was jumping up and down and pawing at the ground. 'Are you in danger again?' asked Finn, and Eder scrunched. 'Can we hide?'

Eder didn't scrunch.

'So we need to run?'

Eder scrunched.

'How much?'

Eder scrunched three times.

'That much? Okay, I know what we'll do. Can your father run?'

Eder scrunched.

'Can he leap?'

Eder didn't scrunch.

There was another cuckoo call, much closer now, and it was answered with whoops and grunts as the baying pack all picked up the scent and closed in.

'Of course I can leap!' oinked Aitor indignantly. 'I may be old, but I can outleap you any day.' He pushed Eder out of the way and stood in front of Finn. 'Eder, how do I say yes?'

'You scrunch your snout, Dad.'

'Ingenious,' said Aitor, and he scrunched. Only as it was the first time he'd ever scrunched, it didn't quite work.

Finn leant down to Eder and whispered, 'I can't understand him . . . is he saying yes?'

Eder scrunched and Finn grinned. 'Okay then. MacGregor's Leap it is. Ready, everyone?'

A wild boar suddenly slid over the wall of the cemetery, his tusks glistening and his eyes wild with the chase.

'Finn!' shouted Eder, at the same moment as Tor shouted 'Dad!'

And then the boar landed on the wet grass, skidded and crashed into the railings surrounding the tree.

'Time to go!' said Finn, and they set off, Eder following close behind Finn, Aitor running on Tor's flank and matching him stride for stride as Tor guided him by keeping up a low whisper.

They raced through the wood, swerving to avoid the trees, going as fast as they could and doing everything they could to stay ahead of the chasing pack.

'Son?' said Aitor.

'Yes, Dad?'

'This leap we're about to do?'

'Yes?'

'Big?'

'No,' lied Tor.

'Liar. What are we leaping over?'

'A river. Wide-ish.'

'Tell me when?'

'I will. I'll count down in strides, three, two, one leap! Okay?'

'Good. Now listen. If I don't make it across—'

'You will.'

'I know, but if I don't . . . Just tell your mother I love her?'

'I told you before – I didn't come all this way to find you so that I could deliver a trotting mess—'

And they were out of the wood and in front of them Eder and Finn had leapt and were soaring through the air!

Tor gulped and shouted, 'Leap, Dad, leap!!!!' He only just remembered to leap himself, and he flew, trotters flailing, across the river with the water raging and thundering and crashing as it pounded onto the rocks below.

The whole jump couldn't have lasted more than a few seconds, but to Tor it felt like it was happening in slow motion. He saw Eder and Finn land on the opposite bank, and then he looked to his right, and with a sinking feeling he realised that his dad wasn't going to make it. Aitor was already dropping, and as Tor landed with a thump and shouted, 'Dad, you're there!' Aitor's front trotters landed on the bank, his stomach hit the edge and he was left hanging and gasping for breath, half on, half off the edge of the cliff. As Tor watched helplessly, Aitor started to slip backwards, his face a mask of pain, then his mouth opened and he shouted 'Tor!' once, in anguish, as his head disappeared backwards over the edge.

Out of nowhere two hands appeared and grabbed his trotters.

'Oh no you don't!' said Finn, as he tried desperately to halt Aitor's backward slide, slipping and sliding on the grass, being pulled towards the edge himself, and then Tor and Eder were there, both of them standing in front of Finn, trotters digging in to halt the boy's slide, and then slowly, ever so slowly, the two piglets pushed him back and back, as he hauled the exhausted and defeated Aitor up over the edge and onto the bank.

'Seneschal!' came a cry from the other side of the river. There was a mass of boars there, none of whom had dared to make the leap.

Aitor raised his head but he was exhausted. 'Tor, talk to them,' he said.

'What do you want?' called Tor.

'Give us the traitor! He lied to us. We were promised gold and all we got were berries that made us sick!'

'Why do you want gold? What good is gold?'

'He promised!'

'I'll tell you why he made you look for gold,' said Tor. He stared at his father as he spoke. 'He wanted you to have a purpose. A reason for living. All pigs want that. We are explorers, we are hunters, we need a quest. I came to find my father, and I found the Seneschal. The Seneschal was searching for his sight, and you helped him find it.'

'So can he see now? Is he not blind?'

'No, he's still blind, but he doesn't need to see to be himself.'

'So why were we looking for the cave then?'

Tor sat up on his haunches. 'The Seneschal was your leader, and that meant giving you a purpose. A quest. A goal. Now he is gone, and you must find another leader, a new quest. Who among you will stand up and take responsibility? Who will stand up and be the leader of this proud group of boars?'

One of the boars stepped forward. 'I will be the leader.' Then another said the same, and then another. Soon all the boars were shouting at each other, and quietly and discreetly, Tor, Aitor, Finn and Eder slipped into the bushes and walked away.

'Nice speech,' said Eder to her brother.

'Hasn't done much good,' said Tor.

'Told you they weren't very bright,' added Aitor, smiling as he limped on.

'You all right there, Dad? D'you want a rest?'

'Do you know what?' replied Aitor. 'I really want to get to the farm. Can we press on?'

'Of course. Come on, Edds, you lead the way.'

Aitor coughed. 'I don't think Iona's coming with us.'

Tor looked at his sister in alarm. 'What?'

Eder shook her head. 'I'm going to stay here.'

'But what about the farm?' asked Tor. 'What will I tell Mum?'

Aitor turned to Tor and waved his snout towards Finn. 'You tell her about him, about the boy. She'll understand.'

Eder rushed over to her dad and nuzzled him frantically, then she turned and came over to her brother. 'Going to have to break our chumship, I'm afraid.'

'Typical. So unreliable.'

They grinned at each other.

'Will you come and visit? I'm sure Finn would love to see you.'

'Might do, if I've nothing else on.'

'When did you ever have anything on?'

'All the time. I just don't go on about it.'

'Fair. Look after Mum?'

'I think Dad will take care of that. See you around . . . Bushy.'

Eder waved her beard proudly, turned away and walked back towards Finn. When she reached him she nuzzled at his pocket and pulled out the handkerchief with her name written on it. Finn beamed at her as he tied it round her neck again. Then she turned back and grinned at Tor. 'You know that speech? All that quest stuff?'

Tor grunted.

'You're actually not as stupid as you look.'

Tor set off with Aitor following him.

'You're going the wrong way,' called Eder.

'I knew that,' said Tor as he changed direction.

Chapter 15

The Northern Lights

On Christmas Eve morning, Tor and Aitor arrived back at the farm. They spotted Heather sitting on the lawn at the front of the farmhouse eating an apple. *Jupiter, a cross between Cox and Starking, with a clean, almost acidic flavour, and firm, dense flesh.* Although she was up and about, Heather hadn't ever fully recovered from the accident in the pool, and spent quite a lot of time snoozing and hanging out with Isla.

She was just savouring the apple and marvelling at how it achieved such a good balance between acidity and sweetness, when she heard something she had feared she might never hear again.

'Hello, Eder.'

Heather's heart leapt in her chest. 'Aitor. You took your time,' she snuffled happily.

Aitor's heart also swelled as he heard the voice he'd been thinking about every day for the last two years. 'Sorry about that, I got a bit held up.'

'They found you then?'

Aitor nodded. 'There's a lot of their mother in them.'

'Quite a lot of their father too,' replied Heather. She turned to Tor. 'Hello, love, welcome back. Where's your sister?'

'We left her in Perthshire. She's safe and really happy. I can't explain it, except to say that she's found her Isla. If that makes sense.'

Heather smiled and then nodded sadly. 'She's got

the omelette and I've got the empty eggshell. I've never known exactly what that means, but Isla said it once about her friend Millie when she moved away.'

At that point Isla emerged from the house carrying a compost bin full of carrot and potato peelings.

'Nikki's trying to make carrot soup, but she's not very good at it so she keeps having to peel more and more.' She saw Aitor and knelt down in front of him. 'Hello, who are you?'

She looked at Heather standing next to him, and then she grinned and started flicking through her phone. She got to one picture and stopped. It was a close-up of Heather with a baby Tor and a baby Eder when they'd just been born. She held up the picture, looked at Tor, Aitor and Heather and then burst out laughing.

'That clears up that mystery then! Where on earth have you been hiding?' She put down the bucket of peelings and sat down with her legs crossed. The pigs immediately got stuck in while Isla chattered away about Nikki and her dad and jam and the farm.

Then she stopped, and looked thoughtfully at the

happily munching pigs. 'My friend Millie's here visiting from Brazil and we're going to go to Colonsay for Christmas and Hogmanay. I won't be gone more than a couple of weeks, and I wasn't even going to mention it, but something makes me think I should say something very important, right now. A sort of Christmas message. Bit like the Queen, I suppose.'

She leant forward and stroked Heather's ears. Heather swallowed her carrot and snickered happily. Isla put her hand under Heather's chin and tilted it up so she could look into her deep brown eyes.

'Heather Duroc, you are, and always have been, the best four-legged friend any girl could ever wish for. I said goodbye to you when I went to London and I cried all day. I said goodbye to you every time I visited you in the zoo and I cried all the way home. When you came back here I vowed we would stay together, and I would never cry because I'd had to say goodbye to you ever again.'

Isla gulped. The lump in her throat was getting bigger by the second.

'I'm sticking to that promise, and even though I

don't know why, I just need you to know that. Because what I've learnt is that we'll always be together. However, whenever and wherever.'

She leant forward and gave her friend a massive hug. Then she jumped to her feet and ran, a slightly wobbly 'Happy Christmas, Heather Duroc!' drifting back, and suddenly Heather was a young piglet watching her eight-year-old best friend tearing down the path to catch the school bus as she had done for so many years.

Heather couldn't be sure if Isla had looked back when she ran off, as for some reason her own eyes were a bit blurry, and she had to dry them on Aitor's beard. She shook her head and butted Aitor happily. 'Come on, then,' she said. 'I need to introduce you to the others. Tor, the children are doing PE with Alastair – I think he's making them run around the ten-acre field. Could you go and get them please?'

'Sure thing, Mum,' said Tor.

That Christmas was the best there'd been on the farm for years. All the animals were overjoyed to finally meet Aitor and, although they were sad that Eder wasn't with them, everyone understood. They laughed and laughed as Tor and Joey acted out their antics in the hotel for everyone, and Aitor pretended to be Eder as she addressed a cave full of gullible wild boars and sent them all charging off to eat deadly nightshade berries.

'We don't usually make much of Christmas,' commented Heather happily as she and Aitor snuggled up on Boxing Day. 'Hogmanay's the big one. That'll really be a party.'

'Hogmanay? Is that a special festival invented for pigs? Hog . . . ? Get it?' Aitor chortled happily as Heather rolled her eyes.

'That is your worst joke ever. Hogmanay is Scottish New Year. Don't know why it's called that – I'm sure Rhona's told me, but I've forgotten. We have loads of food and then someone has to do the first foot with the coal. Oh, it can be you this year. You have to stand outside, and then at midnight you knock on the door and bring in a piece of coal in exchange for a drink. It has to be a tall, dark stranger because if you're blond it means you might be a Viking and they cause trouble. Then we all sing *Auld Lang Syne*.'

'I can't understand a word you're saying,' said Aitor. '*Auld Lang Syne*? I don't even know what language that is.'

Heather started to sing:

> '*We twa hae run about the braes,*
> *And pu'd the gowans fine;*
> *But we've wander'd mony a weary foot*
> *Sin auld lang syne.*'

'Nice,' said Aitor grudgingly. 'What does it mean?' Heather snuggled closer and quietly whispered into Aitor's ear:

> '*We two have run about the hills,*
> *and pulled up the pretty daisies,*
> *But our feet are tired, we've wandered far,*
> *Since long, long ago.*'

Sure enough, the Hogmanay party went on all night and all the next day, so it wasn't until a week or so later that Heather and Aitor said their goodbyes and set off to be alone together.

They walked for an hour or so to a spot that Heather knew, where the earth fell away and it felt like you could see for ever. They settled down on their tummies, sheltered by the tree, and watched the sky. The Northern Lights were raging, an awe-inspiring mix of colours all warping and shifting as they broke across the sky – pinks, oranges, purples and greens.

Heather was entranced. What pig had ever been happier?

'Eder!' barked Aitor by her side.

Heather grinned. 'So impatient. What now?'

'Describe it to me. Paint me a word picture.'

Heather thought for a moment. How could she describe this? Honestly it was like nothing she'd ever seen. Or tasted. And those were her two main ways of describing things.

'Shut your eyes.'

'Eder, I'm blind.'

'Do as you're told. Shut your eyes, tight, tight, tight. Have you done it?'

Aitor nodded.

'Good. Me too by the way. Right, now you've got to imagine little Eder and Tor. Don't picture them as piglets, picture what you feel when you're with them. Got that?' Aitor grunted. 'Now add colours. Can you remember colours? That's what we're looking at.'

Aitor sighed happily. 'I'm tired, Eder. It was a long walk, shall we sleep?'

'Snout to snout?'

'Not this time, Eder. Stay by my side.'

The two pigs lay side by side, their eyes closed, their hearts beating together. From out of the blazing northern lights it started to snow, great fat flakes, falling silently and covering everything in a beautiful white blanket.

'Shall I tell you one last story, my Eder?'

'Okay. Better be a good one though. Like that one you told me about the plant on the hillside that turned out to be heather. I liked that one.'

'Long ago, Nanabozho created the Earth. He gave life to all the animals and the humans and he told them he had made the Earth a paradise where they could live a happy life. Then, when his work was complete, he retired to live in the very north of the world. Once he got there he built mighty fires in the sky to remind his people that they will always be his children, that he will always be with them, and is always thinking of them . . .'

A few miles to the south – on a farm where they made jam and jelly – a clever goat, a celebrity-obsessed Jack Russell, an energetic sheepdog and a lot of puppies were all watching the sky. They were talking about Heather, the four-legged friend who had brought them all together, each one of them with a funny story to tell and a memory to share.

On the island of Colonsay, a girl was sitting eating baked beans out of a tin and playing with a coin on a string that hung round her neck. There was something niggling she felt she had to think about, but it was a sad thought, and right now she didn't feel sad. So instead she gazed out of the window at the cascading colours in the night sky and thought about another night a long time ago. A night when she and her two best friends had sat in a fort made of hay bales, eating apples and chocolate biscuits, and anything had been possible.

Still further south, a piglet was lying in a tree and gazing up at the same fires in the sky. The lights were reflecting in her eyes, flashing and sparkling as she lay on her back, trotters up, thinking about her parents. Next to her, under a blanket, a boy called Finn was chattering away about his own dad, and how, when he was older, they would both set out and find him, wherever he might be. So Eder thought, and Finn talked, and up above them the sky weaved colours so amazing that they made even the stars look ordinary.

And the lights were dancing above another pig as well. Tor was sitting by the river, gazing out at Bennachie, as it thrust out of the landscape like the fin on a dolphin's back. Tor had already thought about his mother – he did that quite a lot these days, and now he was thinking about a time long, long ago. He could almost hear the distant clangs and mist-shrouded skirl of the pipes as the kilt-clad Caledonii rattled their swords and prepared to do battle with their Roman enemies at the foot of *Mons Graupius*. Only this time it would be different, this time the Romans would be overwhelmed by the surprise attack on their flank of a battalion of armoured wild boars, led into battle by Sir Tor, their courageous leader. Half-Bearded pig, half-Duroc, all outlaw.

223

Heather smiled. 'Is that what they are? Are the Northern Lights Nananaha's fires?'

Aitor nodded. 'Nanabohzo, God of the Algonquin Indians. Creator of worlds. Shall we go and see him together? One more migration, Eder?'

'We're not Indians. Will he mind?'

'No. He likes pigs too.'

Heather got up and nudged Aitor to his feet.

'Come on then. Otherwise he'll have eaten all the apples.'

As the snow fell, the two pigs pointed their snouts north and started walking.

Epilogue

Someone else was also thinking about Heather. It was Kirstie, the hard-working chicken, who was still circling the tree, staring at the moths and concentrating really hard. As the lights in the sky blazed, they reflected off the falling snowflakes, creating hundreds and thousands of tiny drifting bursts of white light and colour.

'Och, it's so annoying,' tutted Kirstie to herself. 'I cannae see what direction the moths are flying because of the bothering Northern Lights.'

She walked around the tree and looked the other way, the Lights now behind her, the southern sky dark and full of falling snow. Suddenly a huge grin spread across her beak and she spun round and looked forward at the majestic sight ahead of her, the Lights shimmering and winking as they bathed the sky in colour.

'Northern Lights . . . Kirstie Macgillivray, you're an eejit!'

The snowflakes were falling really thickly now, and from over by the barn she could hear snatches of noise as the puppies and the others rolled in the snow, whooping, barking and laughing. Clucking with delight, Kirstie shook the snow off her wings and ran to join them.

'Guys, guys! I've finished the homework! It's so simple! You can use the Northern Lights!'

Don't Be Pig Ignorant!

Learn some interesting facts about pigs . . .

Heather is a Duroc pig. That means she's red all over, from her snout to the tip of her tail. As you'll know from the book, Heather is loyal, hungry, a great friend and quite chatty. But unfortunately she's not *that* clever. Which is strange, because most pigs are super-clever. In fact, **pigs are the fourth most intelligent animals on the planet** after humans, chimpanzees and dolphins/whales.

Pigs are everywhere. **Pigs live in six of the seven continents of the world.** Can you guess the only continent that isn't home to any pigs?

Did you know that **pigs love playing football**, listening to music and being massaged? Mother pigs (sows) sing to their piglets when they're feeding them. In fact, it's fair to say that although pigs are a breed of animal who may not do very much – we can't use them for milk, like cows or goats, or make wool from their coats, like sheep – **pigs absolutely just love being alive.**

Can you **guess how many pigs there are in the world**? Go on. Have a guess. Answers at the end!

Pigs cannot sweat. So the expression 'sweat like a pig' makes no sense! In fact, they roll about in mud to keep cool. They can also get very badly sunburned so the mud is like putting on SPF50 sun cream – it keeps them safe.

Pigs are omnivores – that means, like humans, they eat everything. Meat, vegetables, plants or, in Heather's case, apples. They have 44 teeth, which is more than us – humans only have 32. And they really like to drink water. **Some really thirsty pigs can drink up to 14 gallons of water every day,** the same as drinking 112 pints!

You know how much Heather likes her food, but do you know why? Humans and pigs have things called taste buds in our mouths that help us tell apart the different flavours in the types of food that we eat. Humans have 9,000 taste buds on our tongues, in our cheeks and on the top bit of our mouths, which is called the palate. 9,000! That's a lot. But **do you know how many taste buds there are in the mouth of the average pig?**

You might not think that pigs are very fast runners, but actually **pigs can run a mile in about six minutes.** Humans normally take about seven or eight minutes to run that far.

Pigs dream like humans, and when they have sleepovers, their favourite way of sleeping is snout to snout.

When sows have piglets they usually have about twelve at once. That's quite a lot, but see if you can guess what was the largest ever number of piglets born in a litter?

Turn the page to find out the answers . . .

ANSWERS

Pigs live in every continent in the world except Antarctica.

There are over 2 billion pigs in the world.

Pigs have 15,000 taste buds.

The most piglets ever born in a single litter was 37.

Have you read all of Heather's amazing adventures?

Available from all good bookshops and in ebook

Find out more at

www.piccadillypress.co.uk

PRESS

Thank you for choosing a Piccadilly Press book.

If you would like to know more about our authors, our books or if you'd just like to know what we're up to, you can find us online.

www.piccadillypress.co.uk

You can also find us on:

We hope to see you soon!